THE **Lake**
Library AND THE

THE Lake AND THE Library

S.M. BEIKO

ECW PRESS

Published by ECW Press
2120 Queen Street East, Suite 200, Toronto, Ontario, Canada M4E 1E2
416-694-3348 / info@ecwpress.com

This is a work of fiction. Names, characters, places, and incidents either are the product of the author's imagination or are used fictitiously, and any resemblance to actual persons, living or dead, business establishments, events, or locales is entirely coincidental.

LIBRARY AND ARCHIVES CANADA CATALOGUING IN PUBLICATION

Beiko, S. M.
The lake and the library / S.M. Beiko.

ISBN 978-1-77041-057-2
ALSO ISSUED AS: 978-1-77090-384-5 (PDF); 978-1-77090-385-2 (EPUB)

I. Title.

PS8603.E42844K35 2012   jc813'.6   C2012-907522-1

Editor for the press: Jennifer Hale
Cover design and photo-illustration: Erik Mohr
Interior images: Due Date Card © JMB - Fotolia.com / Stamp © Liam McCabe
Author photo: Courtney Rae Jones
Type: Troy Cunningham
Printing: Trigraphik | LBF   5   4   3   2   1

The publication of *The Lake and the Library* has been generously supported by the Canada Council for the Arts which last year invested $20.1 million in writing and publishing throughout Canada, and by the Ontario Arts Council, an agency of the Government of Ontario. We also acknowledge the financial support of the Government of Canada through the Canada Book Fund for our publishing activities, and the contribution of the Government of Ontario through the Ontario Book Publishing Tax Credit. The marketing of this book was made possible with the support of the Ontario Media Development Corporation.

 Canada Council   Conseil des Arts
for the Arts   du Canada

Canadä

 ONTARIO ARTS COUNCIL
CONSEIL DES ARTS DE L'ONTARIO

50 YEARS OF ONTARIO GOVERNMENT SUPPORT OF THE ARTS
50 ANS DE SOUTIEN DU GOUVERNEMENT DE L'ONTARIO AUX ARTS

 Ontario
Ontario Media Development
Corporation

PRINTED AND BOUND IN CANADA

MIX
Paper from
responsible sources
FSC
www.fsc.org   FSC® C107923

For my mother — the original dreamer

She walks barefoot through the town. Her senses are lit up in a way she no longer thought was possible. The crisp smell of earth beneath her fine-boned feet. The wind tugging desperately at her robe, her brittle hair, hair that shone gold only a year ago, now hanging limp and white. Her legs had forgotten just what kind of effort it took to get to the lake, especially the climb up the rocky hill to get a good look above it. She's had to stop to rest a number of times already. The wind is still clawing at her, trying to get her to turn around. But she can't. Not now.

She hasn't been here in a long time. When she considers the way things have turned out in the last year, she realizes she hasn't really been anywhere in a while, that her wallpaper and pillow have been her only bits of engaging scenery. Surrounded by doctors and household staff — that is when she felt most alone. But here, on a cliff above the lake, watching the surface of the water bristle and break as the breeze churns the surface, she feels like she's in good company at last. She raises a hand in front of her, reaching, making it level above the water, pretending for a moment that she's floating. And what she's dreamt of for months from her sickbed in a tangle of despair and guilt, it's there, right there. And so is he. It's all she'll ever need.

She takes a step. Then another. And another. She is still reaching.

DATE	ISSUED TO
	CHAPTER ONE

C anvas. Brush stroke. Palette. The light caught the colour and made a clever shade, and I painted on. My work was trying too hard to be a masterpiece, and I was too impatient to let it become one.

"Do you know where you're going yet?"

I looked up from my canvas. Tabitha blinked once, waiting, expecting an answer.

I blew a strand of hair out of my eyes, ignoring the glassiness of hers, and I shrugged. "Northeast. Winnipeg, to start. Maybe Halifax, someday. Basically as far away from the prairies as we can get."

I glanced at Tabitha's shoulder, which was quaking from strain. She'd been bravely holding the same pose for half an hour. Clad in a set of old drapes, striped socks, a puffed crinoline, and a promise, she swallowed back what I didn't realize then were tears, a bodily fluid forbidden by her personal code of casual humour. Though she stood with dubious integrity, with *conviction*, she blinked hard.

I was leaving, and this time, Tabitha couldn't follow me.

"You just want to get away," she sighed through half a laugh. "From *me*."

I was already on my feet, twisting the easel into the dimming sunlight, letting the summer air dry the colours, as Tabitha slumped down to the edge of my bed, her long would-be model's legs vanishing into the folds of endless gauze. My arms were instantly around her shoulders. I chewed the inside of my cheek, but I had no sage words or scraps of poetry to convince her she was wrong.

"There's still the summer," I reminded her. "Loads of time! And it's not like I won't come back to visit. Like I could forget you guys!"

"Then why did you always want to leave so badly?"

I nudged her shoulder with my forehead, biting the inside of my cheek even harder. What kind of answer could I have given her? *I need to get out and go, find somewhere just for me. Treade isn't it. I need a field of sunflowers, a hill to roll off, a sea to be swept away by instead of docked at.* Sixteen is the age when you don't know what you want.

"Just for a change, that's all," I said. "For something . . . *else*."

We sighed and contented ourselves with the gold foil rays escaping out the window. On the canvas, there danced a princess in the stars. Her eyes were shut indignantly, gladiolas and lilies and birds in her hair. I don't think she knew which way to turn when the next dance step came, even if it meant falling out of the frame.

"There's still the summer," we agreed at last.

· ○ ● ○ ●

"We're leaving."

That was how my mother had told me. Needless to say, I barely made a tremor on the sofa as she stood in the doorway, cigarette smoke dancing around her head in a halo. The statement formed a weight at my mother's mouth, and lifted one from my chest.

"Leaving. Really? Like . . . really, really."

"Really, really," she smiled, the gap in her front teeth making a shy appearance as she butted out in her bronze ashtray. "I've already applied for a transfer from Treade General."

We are leaving. My mind exploded in a supernova of *yes.* I did not need the withheld explanation for *why.* My already overtaxed imagination did not require a *where.* My face worked and worked, but I couldn't shave off the grin.

"*When?*"

"At the end of summer, just in time for school." Forever trying to be practical. But she was grinning, too. I knew she wanted to get out of Treade just as much as I did. We crowed and plotted, and as the realization that we were finally going to make our escape bloomed under my rib cage, it was a Goldilocks moment: it felt *just right.*

Ten years we'd wasted in this sullen landscape, and my feet had been itching to run wild from it the entire time. There was no magic in Treade that I saw — there probably never was, even though my desperate eyes turned over every rock to find it. I only saw the town's bitter, broken spirit deriding me constantly through the billowing fog above the Maczik family's ethanol plant. I saw rusted echoes of ghosts in garden gates, ghosts long gone and pleased by it. Their only legacies were inherited sneers, flaking buildings, and deep shades of grey stained into the prairie false fronts. Treade felt like a mannequin, a stand-in for something alive. I saw no chic, rocking jive or sweating drummers, no sidewalk jewel shops, surfing princes, or ancient tales that could shape me into something otherworldly. Treade was so far from the adventure I longed for when we moved here. A vacuum for dreamers.

Abandoned farm buildings were all that was left to house fifty-year-old good intentions. The original town hall stood empty, boarded up and ignored by those who walked by it. The short and often impassable Main Street started with nowhere and ended with a single, dangling stoplight. Treade hadn't recovered since the Depression, and it was clear that everyone should have abandoned the place when they had the chance.

On the western edge of town, just past the spillway, the sprawling ethanol plant was the destination towards which every high school student had pointed his or her compass. That was their end. But not mine. I could see further than that dingy factory, deeper into the world beyond the white fumes above it. Ahead and away was the only place I could look, because there was nothing to see in Treade. The town had forgotten its history, its own *spirit* somehow, and what fragments it still recalled went unspoken like the punctured memories of an Alzheimer's patient. With its rain, its dusty bracken, darkened doors, and feverish youth, a town could never have been more wrong for me. For *us*.

And we were leaving it behind — *at last*. At long, deserved, light-on-the-horizon, holy-Lord-run-for-the-hills, my-life-is-finally-going-to-begin last. Treade would be just a memory filed away, and everything would be different.

It was different, too, when Treade was just a dream and I could shape it as I wished. When I was six years old, my mother had come to me — the then cosmic kindergartner — with her broken heart, jittery nerves, and wanderlust. "We've just got to go," she had said. "There's a whole other world out there, sweetie, made of flickering stardust, and we have to capture it for ourselves." And before my flitting, still new-born perception could adjust, I was cruising in our getaway car, my Care Bear backpack stuffed to the gills with crayon drawings of Alice falling down the rabbit hole into Xanadu (because all of these varied worlds, to me, were connected in their own way). Although I didn't get it, didn't know what was ahead, she held me tight, nose to nose, and that was another Goldilocks moment. Just right.

And I didn't ask the *why* then, either. But I should have.

Adventure, escape. There has to be something out there just for me, little Ash thought. It's hard to be disillusioned when you're six and your entire world is saturated with Disney movies and dreams being wishes my heart made. I saw the world as changing, the kaleidoscope shifting to show bright possibility. It was going to be magical.

But Treade was not the Wonderland I was promised. When I asked Mum later what *really* brought us here, maybe a bit too late, she just laughed, her grey eyes gleaming, cigarette in one hand, smile full of mischief and maybe regret. *Adventure,* her eyes said. *Escape.*

But those things weren't to be found in Treade. Not by a long shot.

"It's by the sea," Mum had said. I believed that, too. Beyond the Firebird's windows, as the grainy desert shifted into a grassy one, I waited patiently for ever-stretching tides whispering mythic gossip to the shore. *By the sea.* She always said we would go there. She used to say that the wide and rolling waters were the world's last freedom, cradling the continents and singing lullabies to the stars. The sea outlived us all, she said, and like us, it couldn't be owned. Our own oceanic blood sang in harmony with these myths. We were nomads; we left and were left, and we preened in the wisdom of moving on.

The way my mother spoke, the smile in her eyes — oh, she could make me believe anything. Make me believe there was magic in Treade, that it was by the sea we craved. Instead, we found ourselves transplanted into a small Manitoba town that was dotted with a craggy lake and a single trafficlight that barely blinked. At the time, I smiled my two-front-toothless grin, and though my mother had lied, I believed Lake Jovan *could* be the sea. I believed we had made it to the promised waters of our dreams.

And deeply, readily, Mum even believed her own words. She needed to — needed *me* to — and with a blood bond no outsider could make sense of, we understood each other without question. We were not born to stay still for long. Wherever we belonged, it was never where we were.

But we had stood still long enough. Finally. *Finally.*

"We're leaving," she had said.

Two words. And I believed her.

DATE	ISSUED TO
	CHAPTER ONE
	CHAPTER TWO

The summer had not been much of one, the overcast sky showing little remorse for several days. Instead of being inspired by the sky, we had to make do with the clouds we were given.

The park near my house contained a wooden play structure we had romped on when we were younger, which was the time when climbing and scraping and yowling "I'm the king of the castle" was most important. It was in the process of being dismantled now, like so much of Treade. Wood wasn't safe, apparently, and no one would risk a broken crown, even though the risk itself had prepared us for the real world.

We had spent the afternoon lying companionably in the park considering these lofty jungle-gym philosophies, head to head amongst empty pop bottles and balled-up Saran Wrap. We'd just had our way with Cokes and Nutella sandwiches, and having exhausted the argument about the merits of glam rock (Tabitha) vs. string theory (Paul) vs. Coleridge (me), we contented ourselves in the silence, trying to claw our way through the tightly knit grey above us. Every day, every conversation, every laugh or petty musing that passed was fraught with the reality we were trying to deny: I was leaving. And that this adventure, that trek, or this picnic could be the last one. The Summer of Lasts, we called it.

And then I sat up like a bolt when the conversation lulled, trying not to give the others any kind of chance to start grieving in their heads. I slapped the grass off my knees, and was already wheeling towards the chain-link fence at the end of the baseball diamond, beckoning over my shoulder. "Let's go!"

Paul and Tabs flanked me as we reached the cut in the fence that led into Wilson's Woods. Beyond was a little beaten path littered with bottles in the brush and rabbit crap at the edge, but we sidestepped all of it and kept going, the sun — wherever it was — at our backs. Boys brought girls here in an attempt to buy romance with a badly rolled joint or a beer stolen from their dads' fridges. We didn't bother with such trifles. We had another agenda.

"I think the last time we were here was the time Tabs nearly died." Paul grinned crookedly, pushing his glasses up. Tabitha gave him a shove.

"I still say there was someone or something in there that day. We should have sacrificed your scrawny body to it."

I laughed at the way they joked, playful, easy. I was usually the one opening up the day with some witty retort, and it made the three of us fit. And soon it'd only be two. At least they had each other.

As we walked, my mind was racing elsewhere, sketching out the possibilities on the blank canvas that lay at the end of that horizon of mine. It was a bad habit, projecting myself away from them when we had so little time left, but I couldn't help it. I currently had this preoccupation with all the things that being in Treade had robbed me of. Right now, love stood on the top of the list. The love I'd dug into through countless books, stories, myths. The love that poets sought to snatch from the air in front of them, the kind of love that sang to sing, and so on, and so on. Staring at the ground ahead, catching flashes of foil condom wrappers discarded in the grass, I could vaguely remember the trials of those petty crushes, and I was glad they didn't lead me here. There were football boys, farm boys, weird out-of-towners that never stayed. I never gave them much thought, never sized them up for much, because I knew that what I wanted from them couldn't happen here in Treade. And I knew that *that* kind of love, the kind whose residue was the only thing left in Wilson's Woods, would be as insignificant as Treade itself.

I would go somewhere else where it *could* happen. The butterflies that the thought raised were more like anxious bees in my stomach. I wanted love and all it entailed, and I was convinced that I was ready for it. I'd be away from the suffocating grasp of a self-pitying, withered town. I'd have freedom, and there'd be hope for love yet. My Coleridge soul and Neruda-spurned pulse couldn't be wrong.

Forget about this place, my heart told me as we came up the steepest hill in Wilson's Woods and danced down it into the hard-packed earth. *There's so much for you in the world, and it isn't in this dust-speck town by a false sea that won't take you out unless you throw yourself in.*

The sea. What squatted in the west side of Treade was a pretender to bodies of water everywhere. It was really a large Precambrian lake, one that could have been worthy of the classification, except for all the neglect. Lake Jovan was punctuated by a muggy beach at the end of town, the way to the water hidden by rocks, gnarled trees, dirty hillside, and craggy overgrowth crawling in the sweaty sand. Legend had it that the beach had celebrated a spectacular heyday . . . until the sixties, when Treade lost interest in it. Forty-five years later it had devolved back to the swamp it once was. Strangers in business suits or four-door sedans could remember the long-lost days of hanging there, sleeping there, *loving* there under the buttery sun. They didn't stay to relive these days, though. They turned their cars around, driving back to Winnipeg or Brandon as quickly as they could, Treade disappearing behind them until it was more faded than a memory. I'm sure even the beach had forgotten those days.

Its best feature was the hundred-foot rocky hill overlooking the water like a grim forehead. We were never allowed to go there by ourselves as kids, but we risked the parental reproach for the sake of adventure. It was the most dramatic place in town, and we coveted it as the stage to all our ne'er-do-welling. We used to stand on the edge, pretending we were victims of an evil bandit's tyranny, or that we were criminals ourselves, and this was where we stashed the booty. We staged crusades and battles there — we *grew up* there. Instead of ourselves, we threw bottles and breakables from the edge, too, watching their bodies separate into tiny blinking shards as they struck the stones below. Having gone there recently, we saw that the tradition had been maintained, but not in such a sophisticated way; car parts, beer cans, and discarded shoes marred the old playground now.

When we all started at Treade Collegiate in kindergarten, the three of us gravitated towards each other with our own special kind of longing, each of us dreaming of something we'd find and grow in each other. Tabitha found me over a fresh serving of Crayolas, the *Labyrinth* soundtrack playing in the background. We shared secrets, popped dandelion heads, made our own set of rules, and stood up to the snotty boys who defied us. It was at their mercy that we found Paul, picking up the ruined remnants of his glasses as the other boys scattered, and we took him into the fold. He was just like us — we would all rather dream than live by the rules of anyone else. We fit.

And here we were, beyond all of our dreams, wading across the field of waist-high grass just beyond Wilson's Woods. We'd been lost in silence for the last few minutes, all the jokes and light teasing dried up. Those adventures were long gone and spent, and walking through that grass, we were united in the tangle of our longing. Change was washing away the breakables from the rocks and forcing us to grow up, and unlike the teenagers that had come before us, we didn't like it very much. I wanted so desperately to discover the rest of the world, and for once in my life, I didn't want Tabitha or Paul there with me. I would never, ever say it, but somehow I think they knew it just the same.

And all of a sudden we were there. Our place.

What the bad fence, the scraggly beard of Wilson's Woods, and the waist-high grass sea have been hemming in since who knows when was a building. Barred, boarded up. It had always been this way, ever since we had happened upon it one fateful summer day after Paul stole Tabitha's retainer for "scientific experimentation," and we had chased him all the way there. To us, it was haunting, but to Paul, it had always been a "beaut." At least three storeys high and crawling with Virginia creeper, it looked too small to be a house, but too big to be a shack or a garage. There was just too much *intention* here. It had art nouveau curls and curves, a rose window, and heavy doors like a mouth, with chains for teeth. The windows looked like they had never been kissed by light; the doors hadn't been crossed in years. There was even a front porch, which was where we had decided to stake out, overnight, on Tabitha's sixteenth birthday. She swore she could hear something walking around on the other side of the wall, and when she realized it wasn't Paul trying to freak her out, she bolted. I remembered how, the night after, I dreamed of the place, dreamed I could see inside the windows, but it was dark and filled with water, and there were black shapes floating everywhere.

But this was our palace. True, other kids had found it, hucked rocks at it, probably made out on the porch. But somehow, no one had ever tried to bust or pry their way in. Because there was no way in. It was a one-door fortress, enchanted by a lonely sadness that made anyone think abusing it was like hurting something alive. We respected it. And maybe the building knew that.

Paul stood by, scratching his clean-cut head behind the ear he dreamed of piercing, but never would. "Well, there she is, ladies. Ain't she a beaut?"

Tabitha rolled her eyes. "You always have to Vanna White it, don't you?"

Paul turned up his nose, mock-snoot. "At least *Ash* appreciates me." He looked at me for approval, but he could tell I was looking past both of them. "Ash?"

I pointed. "That wasn't there the last time."

Stuck in the ashen grounds at various stages of decomposition were the usual NO TRESPASSING warnings, HAZARDOUS PREMISES threats, and the promise of CONDEMNED BUILDING

AHEAD. The signs were as faded as their original intentions. This building was as much a part of our fellowship as I was, and they weren't about to stop us. But this new sign might.

THESE PREMISES ARE PROTECTED BY THE LANDOWNER TENETS OF TREADE PROPER ON BEHALF OF GILLESPIE REIT. PRIVATE PROPERTY. TRESPASSING IS EXPRESSLY PROHIBITED.

"They're going to take it down," Paul breathed in reverent regret. "They're buying up the land and building more houses."

It was enough that I was leaving, but this? I scoffed. Another one of Treade's classic jokes. The only carefully curated enterprise in this town was the sloppy erasing of town artefacts. But I didn't blame the new owners, faceless as they were to us. It was only a matter of time, I guess. Former values of beauty were worthless in a coffin, and this place was always one step away. There might have been gardens and life here a long time ago, lovers on a porch swing, a casual secret. But none of that had survived. There was a disappointing gravity in that moment: mortality was real after all. Even the oldest of us didn't last forever.

We took to the porch, trying to peer through the narrow spaces between the decayed wooden slats. Nothing but darkness wheeling in the abyss. Whatever prospector had claimed this land hadn't given half a care to take a look inside, and they weren't about to give us the chance either.

"And another age comes to an end," Paul postulated in his best philosopher voice, feeling the walls.

"Don't say that," I said, zipping my hoodie up higher as the wind came rustling through the grass sea. I put a hand to the chained-up door, which was covered in ornate, leaping carvings that had lost their sharpness, but would never erode. The Fable Door, I had called it. It wouldn't be telling any stories now. The mournful bay of a train engine in the distance reminded us that we were near the tracks, and nearly outside of Treade. It had always felt like another world out here.

Tabitha thrust her hands into her pockets, the sun still cloaked and choked behind an encroaching evening cloud cover. "Garret said he'd really gotten in there, you know. Through some kind of opening in the back."

That woke me up a little. I had forgotten all about that, even though Tabs had told me only a couple of days ago. Maybe I was too far off in "The Life I Was Going to Have" to have paid attention.

We went to check it out. Around the back of the building was a twenty-by-twenty square of a backyard, overgrown, ugly, a dump site for old car shells, railway ties, or the odd tire pit where kids congregated to misbehave. It was hemmed in with trees from Wilson's Woods that the original builders hadn't cleared, maybe for the posterity of the view, or because the owners wanted the privacy. But the owners . . . who were they? Who had brought this place up out of nothing and planted it here? And why? We begged the answers out of every grown-up whose shirt we could tug, but they all parted their hands and said "who knows."

Most of the uncleared trees in the yard had long since fallen over or broken into each other, and when we checked if there was a breach in the building, the walls were sound, the boarded back window untouched. But all of the boards, the bars, the chains, they never stopped us from trying, hoping, that we could get in someday. It probably hadn't stopped generations before us, either, if they were adventuresome enough. But as far as I was concerned, the only people who belonged in there were the three of us.

I sighed. "Unless Garret tries to drive his dad's old tractor through the place, no one's getting in there now." Dave Garret claimed he spent a night there when he came home from the University of Manitoba in the spring. He said there was nothing in there but a raccoon's nest and bird crap. I couldn't let him be right. Every time we came to this building, *our* building, we checked if a way in had been made by someone more shameless, or if maybe nature had taken out its latest fury in our favour. But the building was made of tougher stuff, and it always fought back. We knew deep down that Dave Garret had probably slept on the porch.

"Well, they're going to drive *something* through it in the end." Paul grimaced, trying to keep his head above the disappointment. "Garret might as well be the one to do it."

"But that can't be the end of it," Tabitha protested as we started walking off, touching the porch rail as we went — our own private salute for luck. "If they're just going to tear it down, why don't we just bust in? They can't stop us now!"

I would have usually been right at the helm of the plans that she and Paul started hatching, but something made me turn. I looked up at the high rose window above the porch, one of the only openings without chains or boards on the facade, and felt that the only way in to this mysterious void was to fly. And for a second it felt possible.

Whatever this place was, it belonged less in Treade than I did. Foundation firmly rooted in dying ground, starved for sunlight. But I was so close to shaking off my chains and boards and making my great escape. I wish I could have claimed ownership of the building like I would a genie, using my last wish to set it free. But there was nothing in Treade with powers like that, not for me, and not for this place, whatever it was. It would have to find its own way out.

I turned away from the building's desperate eyes, imagining the windows and doors making a desolate plea for us to switch places. There was nothing I could do. It was in Treade's hands now, a grasp that I'd finally slipped out of.

DATE	ISSUED TO
	CHAPTER ONE
	CHAPTER TWO
	CHAPTER THREE

"In the dream there's the lake. The sky is the colour of solid slate. And nothing moves. There's no wind, no clouds, nothing. Frozen. The trees are like these bent, scraggly plinths in the distance, and I'm wading out into the middle of the water, but the water feels more like still-wet concrete at my waist. I can't remember why I'm out there, but there's just this feeling of trying to find something. But I can't see into the water, can't even really move. All I can do is sink, lower and lower, sucked down into this sludgy quicksand water. And then I look up and there's the moon, turning its face away, doing everything not to look, until I'm totally underwater.

"The world flips over and so do I, tumbling and tangled, sinking further and further, and not really drowning but being pushed. There are hands, grabbing at me, making impressions in my skin, but I sink away and away, until I hit the bottom. I roll over and see above me — see that the surface of the water is kind of *crashing* towards me, and the lake is draining away. What washes up in the end is me, and the building, a little worse for wear, but I hear no complaints. Nothing. Just that same stillness as before.

"I get to my feet. The ground is shaking, rumbling, almost breathing, but I keep going. It's ripping up the foundation, and I can see the boards flapping like shutters. The Fable Door is shuddering, and the chains start pooling in front of it like wet rope. I keep going but, well, all around me the ground is just cracking. Shattering. And turning white, like chewed-up eggshells. But I can't stop looking because the rose window, it folds in on itself, once, then unfolds. Blinking. Like an eye. Then the door opens. And there's a wave . . .

"I can't really remember the rest," I admitted, "but I think it's what you'd call a bona fide premonition. Well, a pretty good sign, anyway, that this'll be a success, don't you?"

"It's pretty crazy, sure." Tabitha shrugged, noncommittal.

This was not the response I'd expected. Not after years of laughing and mock-gasping as we shared our nightscapes, not after the years and years spent dreaming about what could possibly be inside our sacred, precious hideaway, and not after yesterday, for sure.

After our quest I came home, listless and charged at the same time, not really knowing what to do with myself, this weird energy taking over. It was a confused flight response, like when a bird is about to take off but jerks backwards, invisibly tethered. Leaving was important, but these last adventures with my friends were just as vital. So I resolved to keep my head in Treade while I was still here, just a little while longer, for Tabitha and Paul. They had spent the rest of the afternoon scheming about their great caper, our one last adventure and our one and only break-in, while I was lost in other adventures yet to come. The next morning, I realized this was something we needed right now.

So I decided to use this dream to break back into the fold, to develop our under-cover-of-night schemes, and rally for the gang one more time. Something for Treade, even, to remember me by.

But as we sat in silence that afternoon, watching Tabitha's lackadaisical dog twitch in his sleep, I wondered if she'd heard me at all.

"Well, of course it's crazy," I said, trying to even my voice out, "which is why we have to do this. We won't have another chance, and we've waited long enough." I jumped up, striking a pose on the sofa. "This is our moment!"

This was the cue for Tabitha to break into her usual snorts and giggles, giving her an opportune moment to punt a pillow into my face or jump up and join me. I was always leading the charge, and, faithfully, she'd come running in after, bearing the standard. But not this time. Tabitha's face was carved in granite, giving away nothing as she hung back from the opportunity to give even a smile of support. She just leaned forwards, shoulders hunched, not meeting my eye. The sudden rush of blood to my brain brought me back down to the sofa in a flushed heap, and I tried to keep the breathless smile plastered on my lips, disheartened as it was. "Well? You guys were so pumped about it yesterday."

"Well—," she started, but I was diving off the sofa, grabbing for my bag.

"I even threw together some stuff just in case we wanted to really get on this," I said, digging through and producing a rusted crowbar I had found in the trunk of Mum's Firebird, one of those big police flashlights they had given out at school, and rope. I didn't really know what the rope was for. I had thrown everything together without much of a plan; I just desperately wanted Tabitha to see that I was still with them. I looked at her and expected . . . something. Anything. A glimmer of inspiration, the spark I always saw.

She instead turned her head away, frowning. "I don't know," she finally said. "I talked about it more with Paul . . . maybe it wouldn't be such a good idea. Someone *owns* the place now, and everything."

A feeling like a tiny explosion of angry fire ants bloomed in my chest. The two of them were already sharing confidences without me. What had *really* changed their minds? Tabitha was still looking elsewhere, somewhere I couldn't see, and the corners of her long face pinched inward like bad stitches.

"Tabs?" I urged quietly, my hand hovering over her shoulder. "What's going on?"

"It's just. *Urgh.*" She squeezed her eyes shut, getting up and moving to the piano. It was, as usual, crowded with strewn tapestries, cookie plates, and cherubs. *The Lady of Shalott* hung over it, too, mournful on her boat as she sailed away, dying of a broken heart. A lost life.

Tabitha's lips were set in a thin, pink line, but the words finally smashed their way out. "It's just a lot, you know? First you're going, now our building's being torn down. It's a lot to deal with, Ash. Maybe it'd be better if we just let it go and move on. You're moving on already, why can't we?"

I stared, winded. I hadn't seen that coming. I bit the inside of my cheek, fighting the words that wanted to lash back. Tabitha's house, a sacred palace of Renaissance pictures, candelabras, and touch lamps, slid away. Tabitha, I know, wanted to get away as much as I did, and we had always planned to do the big move together. We were twin falcons strapped to a gauntlet, yet somehow I'd managed to extend my wings and snag her with a talon. We used to slam David Bowie's "Changes" into that piano, screaming the lyrics like fools, but now she wouldn't dare. She plonked a single key instead.

"Tabs, what do you want me to say?" It came out in a flat, ridged tone as I smoothed down my jeans. I shrugged, repacking my bag and clenching my jaw so hard I swear my teeth were turning into diamonds. "I just thought doing this would make you guys happy."

"Yeah. Well."

Maybe they were still planning on doing this. Maybe they would do it as soon as I was gone, bust into what was once "ours" and call it "theirs." Maybe Tabitha's only way of getting over this was to stick it to me and have one adventure I'd never be able to touch. Maybe. *Maybe.* The poison thoughts were carouselling through my head, around and around, making me sick, dizzy. But I couldn't even form the accusation, because there wasn't one. She just missed me, even though I was still right there.

A clock toll went off somewhere but the sound was dull. My face was hot and I felt like there was cotton welling up in my ears and mouth. The dog huffed at the sound and quickly went back to sleep. I was on my feet, the corners of my eyes stinging but betraying nothing. *There's still the summer*, I repeated in my head like the mantra it had become. *There's still tomorrow.* I sent this thought with all my brainpower in Tabitha's direction, because I wasn't feeling sorry enough to admit defeat, to cull her sadness. I was selfish, even then.

I pretended to check the time on my phone. "Anyway. I've got to get home. I'll text you, I guess."

She didn't move. "Yeah, sure."

Yeah, sure.

The door shut heavily in my wake as I padded past the front flower garden. The bees were nowhere to be seen on that monochrome afternoon, which made it a little worse. Tabitha had made up something about "bee speak" a long time ago, and true to form we would hum and buzz to try to discover the opening to their hidden honey world. But there was no buzzing now. Just a sad whine beyond the cul-de-sac.

I ground the heel of my hand into my eyes, doing this covertly just in case she was watching me stalk down her driveway from the living room window. *No.* I promised myself I wouldn't get like this, that I wouldn't compromise my escape and be tortured by the what-ifs of the yellow brick road before me.

Each harsh and hard step away from Tabitha's and back to my block was a curse, punctuated by thunder rumbling over-head. I passed the park. Stopped. There was no way you could see the building from here, but I could sense it. Looming in that hidden thicket amongst all kinds of garbage and broken things. Waiting. I stared at my feet, at the cracks in the side-walk where various bugs were running for cover, like I should have been doing. The thunder shuddered above me, and I closed my eyes, the road forking in three separate directions and my heart outlining each.

Paul.

Tabitha had shut the drawbridge to our castle with me moping at the moat. But what about Paul? He lived at the other end of Treade. Ever since he got his license we'd driven everywhere, the short streets becoming our own as Elvis or Simon and Garfunkel or Iggy and the Stooges burst from our lungs and the windows. When the three of us were kids, Tabs and I had each taken turns being chauffeured on the front of his bike; as time passed, that throne became the front seat of his car.

Paul, so wrapped up in reason and dreaming in logic, swam through frequencies and formulas. He had always raptly watched me painting or listened shyly to Tabitha's music. Though he could not charm us through art, he lured us into his world of facts, the romance of history, the allure of spider's webs and ingrown trees. His Wonderland was real. All three of us together were the prism refracting reveries and reason. And we thrived.

But right now, after hearing the strum of Tabitha's cold resignation, I could picture him distinctly. He wasn't at home thinking of adventures yet to be had. He was probably sitting with a fresh set of encyclopaedias in his lap, staring blankly into the void, not absorbing any of the information in front of him. He was wondering, instead, how things would be when I left, when the music blasting from his car windows faded. Not even the flat, stubbled fields of Treade would carry the memory of our sound.

At this point I could taste the musk of the rain.

The second path: home. I slipped into one of my many daydreams, imagining where that path would take me.

I see myself pounding the gravel of the road's shoulder, desperate to get to my place. I'm running over the trestle bridge, past the sickly bright Heritage Village and into the northwest 'burbs. And I'm home. Our house is set back on the lot, hemmed in by the apple trees that dapple the town like the only silent, productive residents. Unfortunate laundry whips on the line, ready for another rinse cycle. I jog to the front door, which I remember painting a brilliant red as soon as we moved here, to mark this place as our sanctuary. It's peeling now, since we haven't had the heart to sand it down and leave it beautiful for the next tenants. I reach for the doorknob. Pull.

Pull *again.*

It's locked. I bang hard, knowing that Mum *has* to answer. Some shrill reply of *Back so soon, wanderer?* will come, and the usual pillar of perfume or the wisp of cigarette smoke will surround us like a curtain. But nothing. Okay. Keys? I drop down, digging through my bag, hoping I had thrown them in. I hear a jingling, keep digging, *yes!* But something strange is happening . . . the keys won't fit in the lock. They're melting, dissolving, and the keyhole is sealing itself up. This can't be happening. A raindrop *plonks* me square in the forehead. I shut my eyes.

I opened them.

I was still on the sidewalk, standing next to the park. The next strike of thunder was so sharp that I flinched, covering my head in case it started raining anvils. I'd considered my options. And though path two may not have been the most realistic, I knew that was just my heart's way of telling me that path three was the only one to take.

The sky opened and the downpour began. I bolted. Not for Paul's, not for my house. I ran to my building.

I was already soaked, but I couldn't stop. I was swimming in leaps, shooting past the torn-down swings, careening down the hill, racing over the baseball diamond, crashing through the trees like a six-point buck being pursued. The feeling of a sudden, personal adventure had saturated my pores, my bag clapping against my side egging me on. Nothing, not bars or boards, piles of chains, trespassing warnings, or even Tabitha's stone-cold heartache could keep me out now. I would show both of them that I was still here, that this one last adventure was ours for the taking.

And suddenly I was there, and even through sheets of rain and wind-whipped branches, the building stood defiantly, sinking deeper into the ground and refusing to be uprooted despite the onslaught the sky intended. I caught my breath and lunged for the porch, using the cover to get myself together for the task at hand. I tried, feebly, to ring out my hair, smoothing it back so I could go through my bag of supplies unhindered. I noisily wiped my nose. The crowbar was about the only thing I brought that could make a difference. I weighed it in my hand and gripped it tightly, shouldering my bag. Weapon in hand . . . but where to start? I got up and walked to the Fable Door. Despite my dreams that brought the place to life, in reality the chains and boards kept it shut up tight, and even when I slipped the hook of the crowbar into a loose seam, the barriers wouldn't give. I shouldn't have expected to just walk in the front door, anyway. But the back . . .

The rain pelted down with sudden violence, and the sky shifted from milky to bruise purple. The dark and the wet worked seamlessly to make the discarded garbage and old car husks in the building's backyard look monstrous, like they were reeling back to spring on me at any second. The nearby trees of Wilson's Woods weren't faring as well as the building. They swayed and buckled, bending at impossible angles against the wind. Prairie storms came and went, but I couldn't remember a tempest like this one in Treade. It was like I'd stumbled into an arena where a battle of colossal gods was underway, and I was holding only a crowbar. I was having a hard time even moving against the breath-stealing gusts, and I wondered if the wind could make my own body bend the wrong way, like the trees.

I stuck close to the building's back wall, clinging to the siding until I came up to one of the large bay windows, the boards covering the glass hiding underneath. I hadn't been the first to try this, it seemed. The bottom seam of the boards looked chewed up in the places where other improvised tools had attempted to dislodge them. Someone had even tried battering their way in underneath the window, digging out the wall. I reeled back, tightening my hands and muscles, and gave the worn-in impression a *smack* that reverberated in my veins. Shards and splinters flew back at my face with every hit I tried, but I wasn't going to get in any day soon. I'd have to be at this for weeks before seeing results — which I'm sure the previous attacker concluded before giving this all up and going home, pretending it never happened. As I moved up and tried to work the boards away, my adrenaline started to wear out. What chance did I, with the upper-body strength of a raccoon, have against the elements? Against time? Against this building which seemed to flinch every time I came at it with my crowbar? I eventually lost my patience, beating the remnants of that wall like it had besmirched my name, feeling helpless and alone and soaked, like the world itself was closing around me in a rain-soaked fist.

The thunder hurled so hard above me that I felt suddenly queasy. And after that there was a horrible *crack*, like a symphony of broken spines, and for a second I thought I had done it, thought maybe I'd split the very building in two and it was about to come crashing on my head. I wasn't far off. I had enough sense to turn, pivot, and dive, as one of the biggest and oldest trees on the property came down on my handiwork. I choked up a mouthful of mud once the air came pulsing back into me, and when I turned over, I saw that the giant trunk had cleared my feet by only a few inches. The building was not so lucky.

This was my sign. And for the longest second, as I got shakily to my feet and cleared the muck from my eyes, I thought maybe I had died under that tree, and I was now floating above the scene.

Because the gaping hole in the wall that the tree had just created seemed like a far more impossible outcome.

I crouched down and cleared the busted wall away by the handfuls, kicking the bigger, more stubborn pieces into desperate oblivion. And finally, there it was: my struggle had produced a me-sized hole, big enough to shimmy through, I figured, after measuring its width to my hips.

I got in close and peered inside. It was a tangle of shadows and nothingness, and I could feel a cool breeze reach out and touch my face, almost tentatively, before it withdrew and vanished. But whatever was in there — be it a mound of treasure, a band of misfits, or horrible disappointment — I was meant to find it. It could have been our moment; mine, Tabitha's, Paul's . . . and it would be. I knew it. This would be our last great adventure. They would see that I still cared, was still here for them, one more time before they made more plans without me.

But right now, this moment was mine. And so was whatever else that met me on the other side of that hole. After tucking the crowbar safely inside, I shoved my bag through the hole before getting down on my belly and starting to crawl in.

My hands made it in first, and feeling only empty air as I waved them around, I cleared my head through the hole, then my shoulders, and everything else followed through. I wriggled hard and, after a few seconds of panic at being stuck, and telling myself to *breathe*, I was in.

Still on my stomach, I groped around and found my bag, and as I ransacked it, blindly searching for my flashlight, I couldn't keep my mind off the all-consuming silence. The noise of the horrible storm seemed like it had been absorbed by an ancient sound barrier, and my thick panting sounded like a roar in my ears.

I smacked the flashlight head, wishing I'd bothered to change the batteries before I left home today. It flickered, but wouldn't light. I struggled to my feet, knees quaking from the cold, until I stumbled out into the open, wheeling forwards and expecting to land flat on my face again. Instead, my hands met something square, ribbed, and wooden. My fingertips danced and touched and tried to read what I felt in the darkness, but sudden lightning served my need, instead. There they were: shelves, bindings . . . *books*.

I fumbled with the flashlight, smacking it so hard the pain sang in my hand. I was desperate. Like a spooked horse, it sprang into action, and my small halo of yellow light revealed the unbelievable truth. In front of me were books, mountains of them, of every size and shape I could imagine, caked in dust. The shelves went on for dark miles, and emboldened by how all of this *had* to be a dream, I wandered into the centre of the massive room I'd wriggled in to, finding myself face to face with the huge rose window — the window that, in a dream flash, had been a giant, winking eye. Rain pelted it from the other side, where the real world ended and this one began. I stepped reverently into the dim, rose-shaped light the window cast onto the floor, and I realized what this place was. After sixteen years of dreaming, after a decade of enduring Treade and its deprivation of my soul . . . I had fallen down the rabbit hole and landed in a library.

DATE	ISSUED TO
	CHAPTER ONE
	CHAPTER TWO
	CHAPTER THREE
	CHAPTER FOUR

I swallowed hard and turned around in a slow, full circle, shining my flashlight out to scatter the shadows. Dust and cobwebs dominated the stagnant kingdom, a landscape that seemed to stretch impossibly; on the outside, it hadn't looked this big. And the *books* — it didn't seem like they had an end or a beginning, a head or a tail, and I wasn't about to find either and spoil the magic. The very walls were shelves, with balconies above, bigger case units below, and ladders to climb or slide along the shelves to my heart's desire. There were even untouched, austerely upholstered chairs tucked into reading desks, a place where spectres confessed dark deeds and ghosts cleaved to their books on philosophy, making little use of the green teller lamps covered in capes of cobwebs in front of them. I saw all of these shadows with a new clarity, and so much more than that. Because the more and more I saw, the more this defiant feeling germinated in my small chest: this was *my* place. And with this jewelled key to Treade's defiance in my hand, I could lock it all behind me and leave triumphant. The secret was mine at last.

But it was still a mystery, no matter how haughty I was. Ever since Paul got his first library card, he had tried to dig up any town records, photos, files, anything concrete to find out who the building belonged to (even before we felt it belonged to us). But all we had was poorly constructed hearsay, since the meticulously kept Treade archives had been burnt down forty years back at the hand of the archivist's scorned lover (quite the scandal). So no matter who we asked or how we persisted, we were waved off, shooed away, told to "mind our own business," and some, who were as ancient as the town and too slow to trust, said the place was cursed. That those who had owned it, who had built it, had never even been inside. "Rich folks and their secrets," they said. It was the breeding ground of endings.

Now inside, seeing with my own excited eyes what the walls had concealed all these years, the mystery didn't deepen — it dissipated. All bets were off. We had to start from ground zero, and all of a sudden I could picture the place lit up and alive, imagining that a long time ago there were people who loved this place, who were happy here.

The possibility flickered away in harmony with my flashlight. I smacked it against my palm and moved out of the rose outline, wondering how an entire town could totally ignore this book palace, and realizing that whoever claimed to have sneaked in here had to be lying; no one could have kept this quiet all these years. And the books . . . I trailed my hand from shelf to shelf, the gold foil stamping glittering when I wiped the grime away, the leather spines buttery and supple, too. I felt as though I was the first person to ever touch them, that each time my fingertips brushed across a book that it came to life, shivering to the depths of its saddle-stitching. I felt like I was on a mission to salvage every dreaming heart who stood outside of this building, or in Treade at all, who dreamed of something more.

After giving it another shake, my flashlight lingered dimly over a nearby ladder that soared up a free-standing bookcase. I think everyone who has ever felt that books provide sanctuary has dreamed of sliding on those kinds of ladders, little library birds darting from flower to flower for the hidden nectar at their hands. And I was no exception. Tucking the flashlight in the waistband of my jeans, I gingerly tested the rungs for splinters or faults, but my footing was sure despite my soggy shoes. About two rungs up, I reached out and snagged randomly, coming away with a gold-stamped cover revealing that Percy Bysshe Shelley was here, alive and well. "Death is the veil which those who live call life; They sleep, and it is lifted." Up higher were more of his contemporaries, along with the reams of the poetry I always loved and tried to share, but they were few and far between who could dive into the lines like I could, and swim in pentameter like a wave. Even past the mud caked in my eyebrows or the damp clinging to my clammy skin, I felt like I was being embraced by long-lost family, like I was coming home, and all my years of loving literature and being called out as a *nerd* or a *dork* were wiped away. They gave me strength instead, pulsing their verses into me like currents. So I kept climbing. Hemens, Burns, Wordsworth, Tennyson beckoning to my occupied hands — one clutching the wooden bars, the other browsing. I gingerly wrested each book free, gave my noiseless respect, and shelved it again. And I climbed.

Suddenly, I had come to the very top of the shelf, and the end of the ladder. I chanced a look at the ground beneath me, only once, and I got the instant boomerang feeling of having come too high, too fast. I held on tighter and reassured my drenched feet that I was nimble and safe, and I was just fine where I was. Nothing could hurt me up here. I took my light out of my waistband, shining it around to see if I could find anything else brilliant before I started my descent, and something winked at me from across the top of the shelf. It was bound in bright silver, and it seemed like it had been discarded or simply forgotten where it lay, under a landing and just out of reach. I only wanted to see the title, feel the book's weight in my hands, and savour it. I put the flashlight down on the shelf top and, hooking my ankles into the rung, started to rock the ladder side to side. It was jammed at the bottom and refused to slide where I wanted it to, and I wasn't about to climb all the way back down to move it. Arrogance punctuated my struggle, and I started goading myself on. *Lean out a little*, I thought in a whisper. *You can reach that, come on.* Hands outstretched, ladder creaking underneath me, I gave it one more try. I lunged.

The second snap of the night, and this time not in my favour. As the rung broke underneath me, my wet shoes sent me wheeling in a backwards-forwards dance to get my balance again. I was forced to throw myself forwards and wrap my arms around the top of the shelf, clawing, one foot hanging free and the other still keeping a toehold on the ladder. I couldn't scream — I was too busy trying to summon to my cause every fibre in my muscles to scream — and with one bad shove, the flashlight tumbled to the ground to explode in a rush of glass and metal.

Panic does not begin to describe what went on in my head. My free foot kicked out in the dark, trying to find a place to land, while the other was losing the toehold. I was hanging onto the ladder with my pant cuff caught on the splintered rung, but even that eventually ripped free, and the ladder shot away in the other direction. Very suddenly, very vividly, I could picture the way my bones would break on the way down, marrow slipping out like icy gel to outline my gnarled body. I screamed, trying to keep my waking dream death at bay, and I clenched tight to the bookcase, reining in my hysteria, because I could feel the heavy shelf rocking with every precious movement I had left. I tried to reach for the ladder again with my toe. No go. *I don't want to die, not alone, not in the dark, in a place where no one goes for fear of a curse or because they've just stopped caring.* I could feel my joints popping and my sweaty palms slipping, the pain searing through my white knuckles.

Okay. Just focus. I felt around underneath me with my foot; there had to be a bit of shelf I could plant myself on and use to shuffle back to the ladder. My toe whispered past a bit of wood, a bit of hope. That meant I'd have to let go a little and slide back, gently, so gently, to ease myself onto it. My hands started loosening up, inch by inch, muscles cramping with the effort. One hand caught on something sharp as it moved back, feeling like a bug bite, but I ignored it. I was nearly there, my foothold halfway to secure. The sharp thing on my hand was starting to dig in, to nearly cut the flesh, but I was so close it didn't matter. *Just a little more. A little more . . .*

I lost my grip in one horrible instant, and my weight came down on the shelf too hard, too fast. *Crack* number three, the worst of all. I felt the air grow leaden as I fell, heard books coming free of the broken shelf and smashing to the ground. *Goodbye, Treade. I never had to leave you after all.*

I jerked to a stop.

There was a hand around my wrist. An impossible, truer grip than I could have hoped for. I'd been caught from between the banisters of the landing over me, but it was too dark and I was too scared to look for the hero. All at once I could feel the hand pumping strength into my arm, swinging me back and forth until I could follow the path of the momentum onto the ladder — it was closer than panic had me think. Before I could register a single thought, I was scuttling down the ladder to the safety of the ground, rungs breaking with each frenzied step, until I stumbled and fell mere inches instead of several feet. Amidst the shards of my flashlight and the poor, ransacked books, I was alive.

I caught myself on my hands and knees, but a shock of pain raced up my arm and made me collapse all over again. Whatever had been nagging at my hand on the top of the shelf had burrowed its way under the skin, the pain buzzing all the way to my wrist. Sitting up and poking it as much as the furious pain would allow, my bleeding, sticky hand revealed a huge blade of wood lodged in the wound.

The silence, which had since settled around me like a heavy cape, suddenly burst apart. The sound started low, and for a second I thought it was just the rain, but it became louder, and way more intentional. Footsteps. Frantic ones. Ones that weren't mine. I twitched towards the source, but the echoing steps sounded like a thousand feet at once. This had all happened so fast; nearly dead to alive and bleeding, I didn't stop to think that it could've been my invisible saviour. Instead, it sounded like the racing of an angry guard dog coming to claim the trespasser. My usually vivid imagination had given me enough fuel to make a break for it, and I was on my feet twisting and turning, feeling my way back out and into the world. An ear-piercing buzz made me stop short as every light in the room, lights I did not realize even existed, raged to life, blinding me worse than the dark had but revealing my exit and the bag I'd left behind. I'd pushed it under the small coffee table that hid my hole-in-the-wall, and snatching it up I dove towards the free air.

I had my hands so far out into the opening that I could feel the cool mud beyond. But as I reached, there was a hand on my ankle. Then another, pulling on my skin like it was reeling in the catch of the day. I clawed for my opening, but it was gone, and I was dragged back into the library, the orange light burning my vision to a blur. But I didn't come out feebly; I came out swinging.

The crowbar clanged in my attacker's direction and bounced off the place in the floor where he'd just been crouching. He moved like a shade, a bigger and stronger shade, and he dodged my next desperately inaccurate blow. No sooner than I had got up, I slipped and hit the ground, my weapon spiralling away. I was pinned in a corner with only bookshelves at my back.

"Don't even think about it!" I rasped, trying to keep him at bay with words of completely feigned fearlessness. "Get away from me!"

But he was moving closer as I plastered myself against the wall, leaving a streak of blood pumping from my wounded hand behind me. I was weak despite the adrenaline, and tired. And without anywhere to run, I looked up, tears finally making their coarse cameo. Through them, I saw there was a face above me, the shadows on his features scattering as I looked closer.

Past a curtain of damp, unkempt auburn hair, I saw a boy — well, more a young man — but he held himself like he was uncertain about being the sum of his parts. He stared back at me with eyes like shiny wounds above drawn, worried cheek-bones. I drew my knees up and tried to study him, but I only shivered as he crouched down to his knees, eyes never leaving mine, and started to crawl closer.

"Stay away from me!" I warned again, this time less sure of myself. I unconsciously held my hand out to stop him, and he caught it in a python grip. I resisted, but he brought it up to his eyes and they softened, whatever suspicion had been there pooling at the corners. He looked at me and shook his head, worrisome.

"Just leave it alone, I'm fine!" I pulled my hand back in his moment of pity and cradled it close to my chest. He looked a bit bewildered, but made himself comfortable and started digging around in his pocket, until he produced a beaten-up green tin with a faded cross on the lid. He sidled in a little closer so he could show me the contents: gauze, a small glass bottle of what was probably antiseptic, some hooked scissors, and a big pair of tweezers. I winced and cradled my hand tighter.

"That's nice, but . . . no. Really. I don't need—"

Very gently, he put his hand to mine and held it there. And he looked at me just once, a stare that spoke volumes with his vocabulary of silence, and I relented. I clenched my teeth as he cleaned the blood away, as every poke and prod of his combination scissors-tweezers-pull-repeat made me want to shriek bloody murder and run. But he said nothing as tears pricked my eyes again, just worked in hunched concentration. He kept brushing his curly, disobedient hair out of his eyes, and I realized that he was just as soaked as I was. How he got in, I didn't ask. Who he was, I only pretended to wonder. Right now he was in the middle of saving me for a second time, and I was too quietly awed to be curious or afraid.

Cut, prick, pull, *yank*, and the thing came free. He presented it to me, proud and grinning, my painful performance butting out any chance for a meaningful reply.

"You keep it," I offered. "It can be your trophy." He seemed to laugh but no sound came out. He bound my hand carefully with the rag he had used to clean the wound, and after one last examination, the artist looked pleased with his work.

"Thanks." I sniffled, digging the hand into my eye to get rid of any offending tears.

He smiled, taking the hand and dabbing my cheeks with the bandaged part of it. His touch was a cold surprise. I tried to look away as he helped me up, steadying me and checking for other injuries. I shied away from the fussing.

"I'm fine, really," and suddenly he was only a few inches away from my face, unblinking, staring down into me. Until now I hadn't realized just how tall he was compared to me, at least by a head, and I shrank back. His hard jaw insinuated only a shadow of a beard on that gaunt face, and he wasn't smiling, anymore. I stepped away and into the open, finally composed.

"Was that you up there?" I pointed to the accident site, and he followed my gesture. A nod.

Teenaged ineloquence took over as I fiddled with my bandage. "Oh. Yeah. Thanks."

He looked at me intently as I tried to stop my brain from conjuring some other grim hypothetical had he not come to my stupid rescue. With a look up I finally let myself smile, put aside the hesitation, and held out my bandaged hand. "I'm Ash."

Taking it by the fingertips, he bowed an exaggerated courtier bow, but I didn't get a name. I swallowed, ignoring that he hadn't let go yet.

"Um," I tried, "got a name?"

The smile faltered. He dropped my hand like it was dangerous. After a few seconds, he turned around and wandered off into the stacks. I followed.

"Hey!" My voice bounded through the dusty place as I trailed behind him.

But as the walls opened into the full grandeur of the building, now fully lit, my pace instantly slowed. It wasn't just the number of books. It was because it was less a library and more a palace. Chandeliers hung heavy from the ceiling beams; lamps were buried in sconces lining the walls. The woodwork, though dusty, was dazzling in turns. And a clock ringed in antlers sat silent on the rear wall above the Fable Door (which was as beautiful inside as it was on the outside). It was as though all my dreams filled the shadows in and gave it light.

Out of the corner of my eye, I saw the silent stranger boy cast a fervent glance over his shoulder, unable to rein in a look of distracted longing and fear, as the shadows crept back into the room. And though I saw these things, I was far too enraptured by what I had stumbled into to register anything happening on my periphery. I turned my back on all of it because my brain was still madly trying to unearth the reason behind this place. I was so naive to think that reason belonged in this library at all.

I cocked my hip and twisted around, looking for the boy. "So how did you get in—"

He was gone. The frosted lamps flickered. I blew the hair

out of my face, wiping my nose with my wrapped hand as
I turned around to leave . . . but something grazed my face.
There was a small piece of paper stuck inside the rag. *Must have
been in his pocket*, I guessed. On it were two letters scratched
desperately into the paper:

LI

Then the lights started going out, row by row, following a
distant roll of thunder. I took this as my cue to go; it was suddenly so cold.

Behind me, the clock above the Fable Door started ticking.

He calls upon the Earth, and she responds that she feels life and joy.
She then proclaims, "And death shall be the last embrace of her/
Who takes the life she gave, even as a mother/ Folding her child,
says, 'Leave me not again.'"

She closes the worn book against her hand, a flesh bookmark, and she stares out the window. The gravity of the lake hangs just in the distance, saying something she's been straining to hear for days now, tuning out other sounds the better to listen. She barely notices the doctor amble in, his *tut-tut* preamble about not having left her bedroom in a week pinging in her ears like the dead channels on her radio. These country doctors, remarking on her books, too, like the only one she ought to be reading at this point is a holy one. She humours him with a glance, trying to look demure, but it comes off as vacant. He flashes a light in those eyes and, sure enough, *tuts* again. Then the blood pressure cuff is too big for her arm. She nearly smiles at the doctor's palpable frustration that she's lost more weight, that she's obviously been hiding or just ignoring her food. He thinks the smile is just a tick.

Ruth, the housekeeper, comes in, hands folded in front of her and patient for the verdict. The doctor takes her out into the hall to discuss "proper care," which Ruth should be responsible for. She'll probably just get another tired scolding instead. *You should be watching her more carefully, what she eats and drinks*, and Ruth, stubborn as steel, will retort, *We're doing the best we can, but the lady's gone right off her head since the terrible thing with her son, and right after her husband, too.*

Once their conversation fades to the other side of the house, she climbs out of her chair and the body groove she's left behind. She somehow shambles across the gulf from chair to wash basin, which has been filled and untouched since morning. Leaning over the water, her reflection is pockmarked, rippling. She puts her hand right over the surface, floats it over, lets it sink in carefully. She is not surprised at the lack of sensation. She removes her hand and plants both of them firmly on either side of the basin, anchoring herself to the washstand. She bends, her face whispering into the water like they were two parts joined. She counts. She swallows. She stops counting.

Blackness. Suddenly she's on her back, choking up water onto the country doctor's bloated chest. The dead radio channel finds a signal, and a crackling laugh bursts from her lungs with the water gurgling behind it. "I told you she was off her head, I told you!" Rustling, shouting, and "She can't be left alone—"

"What did you say, ma'am? Calm yourself now, you're hysterical."

"Easier," she repeated, covering her mouth, trying to hide the smile. "It's easier than I thought."

DATE
ISSUED TO
CHAPTER FIVE
PROPERTY OF
TREADE
PUBLIC LIBRARY

I passed through our red door like a ghost, for a second wondering why it was open now, then remembering that it had never been locked; I had only imagined it so. I could hear Mum in the middle of another coughing fit, hacking something up in the upstairs bathroom. I dropped my bag in the hall.

"Mum? Are you okay?"

She poked her head out of the doorway, cigarette in hand as she stared. "You're soaked! And dirty!"

"No, really?" I kicked off my shoes and made to shake off like a dog. She mock-shrieked and bustled down the stairs, grabbing me in a hug and muddying herself up in the process. I laughed, trying to drown out the evident rattling I could hear in her chest as she clutched me to it.

"I know I'm the kid, but you're the one with the bad habits."

She just smiled and made me hand over my muddy sweatshirt. "Worry about yourself for a change. Where were you? Rolling around in the receiving ponds by the plant?"

She moved away, depositing my sweater in the laundry on the way to the kitchen. I was glad she left me alone, because

I couldn't hide the muscles tensing in my face. Where had I been? It was a straight enough question. After I wriggled out into the open, into the deepening dark, I knew that I had walked and walked, but until Mum had asked, I had no idea how my feet got me home. I felt completely detached, like I'd been sleeping, like it was suspended above me but it hadn't happened at all. I do remember looking back though, seeing the building like I always had, except now it looked less solid, like a mirage about to fade away.

"*You* okay?" Mum chided from the kitchen, the kettle clicking off. My mouth couldn't form the words, and the dream memories hung full of holes around me, trying to coalesce into sense, and failing.

I shrugged it off, tried to look convincing, huddled around my mug when she offered it. "Fine," I finally got out. I didn't have the constitution to deal with phantom boys and abandoned libraries right now. I needed to prove it wasn't a dream before I let anyone else in.

"I'm sorry I was out so long, sweetie. I had to take a split shift for the new nurse and had to sign some papers at the real estate agent. Oh, and were you in the garage, earlier? You left the door open, scatterbrain."

I slumped into a rickety chair at the table, letting my lungs deflate through chilly lips. "Sorry," I muttered, closing my eyes and relaxing as the heat of the tea washed through my marrow.

I could feel Mum watching me through her half-lidded eyes, the way she watched her patients while their IVs dripped and they made it through the night. She was looking me over for vital signs, or the lack of them. "Things'll be different soon," she said.

I perked up, forced a reassuring smile. "Sooner the better, right?"

Unable to catch the words from spilling out, I suddenly thought of Tabs. I imagined her lying on her bed with *The Slider* album playing behind her thoughts, dreaming hard of cosmic dancing right out of Treade in my wake. If I could whisper her into a bottle and carry her away with me, I would. But there's no enchantment in Treade, remember?

Or is there? I cast an unsure glance to the bandaged hand in my lap.

"So where were you? Waiting things out at Tabitha's? In the mud?" Mum smiled, her smoker's creases crinkling deeper. Past the smoke, her smells of LypSyl and the lemon disinfectant from Treade General where she spent her days — and most nights — were usually comforting. They didn't help me now, though, just put me on edge as I tried to wake myself up.

A mouthful of tea inspired an evasive reply. "I get the feeling I've ruined the summer for her. Leaving at the end of it, and all." I sighed, because this was the truth, but it wasn't what was at the forefront of my mind.

Mum eased back into her chair, fiddling with her half-blonde, half-mousy locks. "You've been best friends for ten years, sweetheart. It's a hard hit, but she has to learn to deal with change."

I prickled, seeing Tabitha's set mouth when she said she and Paul had made other plans without me, had given up on me without warning. "Well, it's her problem, isn't it? Guess I'll just let her deal with it . . . I'll wait *that* storm out here for a while, thanks."

I wrapped my pruney fingers around the mug, making sure to conceal my bandaged hand behind my back as I groaned to my feet, kissed Mum gratefully, and headed to my room. "I'm going to paint a bit," I lied.

I did a quick shoulder check from the hall. Mum was getting

up to change the radio station, her best friend, her own electric Tabitha. The voices were her confidantes, like the intercom at work that echoed distresses and desires. She'd rather bare her soul at a frequency right now, and she knew I'd rather bare mine at my walls. Her nursing expertise saw my teenaged apathy and treated it with a tried and true dose of silent withdrawal and keep-it-to-yourself. Which suited us fine. She was energy sapped from the demands of managing other people's lives, and I was wrecked from managing my own.

Things'll be different soon, echoed in my skull.

I shut my bedroom door so it barely made a sound against the carpet. I breathed out the mysteries tumbling inside me — the library, the boy — exhaling them in the vinyls hanging on my walls, in the posters and printouts papering the rest. Old concert and play tickets from city trips, cards, notes written in Sharpie; they absorbed my secrets as they always had, with room to spare. My mind fast-forwarded to taking it all down and pasting it on foreign walls.

Keep my secret for me, I asked the room.

Putting down my tea mug on a side table, I sprang from the floor like a haphazard bird, careening to the bed. I flicked the crystals hanging off the night table lamp; beyond them I saw the dancing canvas princess by the window looking resentfully away. I had used elements of Tabitha's face on her, and the result left me wanting to turn the painting the other way.

I looked at my hand. *Li.* I tested the word on my tongue. Or is it a name? Lee? Was that how you said it? Or lie? Li. Li-brary.

I rolled up to the edge of my bed, slowly unwrapping my hand. When the bandage ran out I turned it over. My palm was clean and pink. Nothing there. Not even a scratch.

I shut my eyes, still trying to wake myself up.

DATE	ISSUED TO
	CHAPTER FIVE
	CHAPTER SIX

PROPERTY OF
TREADE
PUBLIC LIBRARY

My Polaroid camera hung from my hip, tapping it as I came to a stop. I fingered the knobs, biting my lip as I scrutinized what I now knew as "the library." The sun winked above me like a lucky coin, goading me on. I didn't know how much further luck was willing to take me after yesterday, so I recited some ground rules to myself before going in: *Be brave. Be careful. And don't climb anything.*

Click click. The processor released a black-and-white Polaroid tongue that I shook before dropping it into my bag. The camera had been a gift from an aunt who once drove all the way to Treade to give Mum a piece of her mind for moving to the middle of nowhere. The camera was to keep me busy. And it would. With it, I could get instant proof that this rabbit hole was real. A digital camera could be tampered with before the evidence was produced. These pictures would be the solid proof that my injured (had it been?) hand had failed to be. I obviously couldn't trust my eyes anymore, that was certain.

Down on my knees, squishing the damp ground underneath, I squeezed through my opening in the wall. The table legs came into focus and the bookshelves, too, but I stopped myself, sucked in a breath, and listened. The lights were on, but I hoped nobody was home. It wouldn't take much for some meddling kids to have discovered my hole and crashed the party. But all was silent. After slithering through the opening, I got to my feet with slow, steel-spring determination. For a second I reconsidered having come alone, but I needed a few things figured out before anyone else followed in my uncertain footsteps.

I sneaked past the lofty bookcase and took a good look around the centre of the room. Everything was meticulous and untouched, barely a grain of dust or a cobweb in sight. The paint and varnish looked as fresh as the day it'd been applied. The lights shone with crystal clarity. In the dark of the storm and the glow of my flashlight, it had looked dingy and unkempt. Had someone been in here to clean house since yesterday? I raised my camera and clicked. My heart valves flapped like wild wings as I wandered further, finger finding the capture button for every little thing I saw. It wasn't long before I stopped collecting the pictures, instead leaving them in my wake to come back to later. Reloading the camera from the packs in my bag became rote. I was too lost in what I saw; the books, the sheer magnitude of the space, all contained and standing away from me with apprehensive beauty. It was like nothing I had ever seen before, and only a trace of what I dreamed of.

Aim and click. I'm suddenly girl-Hansel, Polaroids my bread crumbs in this looming forest whose trees have been pulped and printed. I stopped at the far wall, got a good close-up shot of the antler-bedecked clock, and leaned in closer to see that the antlers were attached to tiny, prancing deer, encircling the mother-of-pearl face. I suddenly realized that the clock's ticking was counting the seconds with my pulse. I pulled out my cell phone, and sure enough, it was keeping perfect time. I leaned in even closer, impulse dictating I touch the clock face to make sure it was really there—

Something flew across the room and smacked the clock just where I was about to touch it. I wheeled backwards, accidentally sending my camera flash in the direction of the onslaught before throwing myself behind a reading table. I breathed hard, looking around wildly and finding no one before I shakily scooped up the last five photos I'd taken.

I shuffled the pile. There was a picture of the curving twin iron staircases snaking up to the library's second level; another of the never-ending row of shelves captured from a strange angle, then two more of the ghostly, untouched tables . . . but I doubled back. There was something crouching behind the staircase, which was very close to my right. I looked from the picture to the stairs, squinting. A shadow. A face.

It wasn't clear enough, though, whatever it was. A reflection of light off a lamp, maybe. I sighed and berated myself for being such an idiot, acting like I was trapped in a Nancy Drew mystery and was about to be set upon by a flock of ghosts. I got to my feet and decided to go after all the pictures I'd left behind.

But after taking one look at where I'd only just come from, I froze. No pictures. How could I have expected otherwise? There was something in these walls slowly eating away at the reality it inhabited, and I'd become a part of it.

A creaking echoed from behind me. I stood mannequin-still, eyes and head swivelling around slowly.

"I know you're there! I'm not stupid!"

My defiance ricocheted through the empty building. When it boomeranged back, it sounded almost as dumb as the idea of coming here alone. I wasn't about to be scared into leaving, though. Not by a long shot. A role reversal of cat and mouse was imminent.

Swallowing my suspicion, I went the casual route, strolling around and taking more pictures at my leisure. With a pause, I glanced back at the ground a few feet behind me. Pictures gone. Of course. I turned and kept on, walking down the centre aisle, aiming up. *Click. Spit. Click. Spit.* Reload. Pause. Turn. Gone. Okay, time for plan B. I started snapping pictures feverishly, stepping backwards as the pile of fresh photos at my feet grew. They didn't disappear, and for a second I felt vindicated.

Almost, anyway, until I backed up into something. Someone.

Whoever it was didn't even give me a fair chance to turn around. There were hands suddenly pinioned around my arm and torso, pushing and trying to pry the camera out of my hands. When I couldn't fight any longer and had to let go of the camera, the momentum of letting go drove me forwards in a half spin. I caught myself. It was *him*.

He experimented with the camera, recoiling and shocked when a picture came out. At that he grinned, aiming it at my face to snap a few.

I lunged at him. "Don't do that! You're wasting film!" I tried to grab it but he buckled backwards with a half step, teasing me, taking more, and dancing away. He wanted a chase, and I was more than willing to give it.

Midsprint, I whined, "Give it back! It's an antique! You're gonna wreck it!"

I skidded to a halt as he ducked around a darker corner. As

soon as I lost sight of him, he was gone, but a few flashes from
above gave him away instantly. He was lazing on his belly on
top of a bookshelf without a care, even for heights, and thor-
oughly enjoying himself.

"Okay, okay!" I shied away behind my hand. "I get the
point; you can stop any time."

He gave a mock-pout, saddened that I wasn't amusing him
anymore, so he turned the camera on himself and snapped
one. While he sat, temporarily distracted by sudden blind-
ness, I scaled the ladder nearest to him, but stopped just out
of arm's reach remembering yesterday. I held out my hand.

"Give it here, whoever you are, and I promise I won't sue
for damages."

He cocked an eyebrow and curled a half smile, those
strange eyes looking for a fair trade but willing to give in. The
camera came close to my hand, and as I wrapped my fingers
around it, he yanked it towards him, bringing me, rolling
ladder and all, right to him.

I shrieked. "This isn't funny, just let go—" But his ice-chip
eyes were concentrated on me, relentless. I wanted him to
just *say* what he wanted, rather than keeping me constantly
suspicious. He was coming in closer, closer, his pupils about
to devour, until he pinched my nose and made a throaty
honking noise before letting the camera go. I rubbed my
nose, disgusted that I fell for it and muttered "Idiot" while
checking the camera over.

He kept watching me like an amused feline, face planted in
folded arms and fascinated as I hung the camera around my
neck. I grappled with my thoughts, still shaken and uncertain
about what was there between us. Impatient with myself, I
finally said, "So I guess you're L-I."

He wrinkled his nose, shaking his head.

"Um. I mean. Li?" I pronounced it "Lee."

At that he looked genuinely insulted. I threw up my hands. "Well, maybe if you just *told me* what it is I wouldn't keep guessing wrong."

He leaned back on his arms, crossing his ankles and looking bored.

"How about 'Lie.' As in li-on?"

He squinted, wrinkling his nose again like he was trying to work out whether or not I was right. Then he made a face like it hurt him to think, and at the end of it all he shrugged, conceding, and gave me a slow clap. "Lie" it was, then. I couldn't dodge my own smile.

"Are you this annoying to everyone who asks?"

Li's grin engaged every muscle and line on his face before he raised his shoulders cartoonishly, again.

"Figures." My mistrust was waning, though. He was just a prankster. Messy, rumpled, partway good-looking in a dogged kind of way, and only irritating as far as he knew it was amusing. But there were still some unanswered questions that were gnawing hesitation into my bones.

He also wouldn't stop staring.

"So . . . How'd you get in here? Did you follow me through the back?"

Maybe we were fellow trespassers, unified under breach of conduct, which made me feel a little less guilty in treading all over someone else's memories. Li didn't bother with a reply, though, now too busy digging around in the breast pocket of his faded wool peacoat to give me a second's notice.

I wasn't about to let it go. "Well?" I insisted, drumming my fingers on a shelf. "Are you going to say *anything* or what?"

A Polaroid suddenly cuffed me square between the eyes. I rubbed my face, and before I could blurt a *"don't"* he was chucking another one. I caught sight of the big pile of pictures he'd scooped up from the library floor, the pile that had started this whole thing in the first place. He flipped his thumb over the edges, back and forth, like he was a hotshot blackjack dealer straight off the tables. Without those pictures, I had nothing to take back with me, nothing to show. He knew I needed them, picking another one and handling it like a ninja star under his thumb.

I dove further up the ladder, defying what happened the last time, and went after him. But Li was already to his feet, flipping over the balcony and mounting the second level like a lemur. He twisted and waved the pile around, flicking one out and snapping it in my direction. *Onslaught occurring, counterstrike!* I ducked as three sailed past my head, and in spite of myself, I laughed.

Despite not knowing him, despite having almost met such a terrifying end yesterday, despite the sheer mystery that cloaked this entire place, I felt like I could be free here, and chasing after Li, wherever he was leading me, was what I needed to do. But when I got to the top of the ladder, I remembered how much I hated heights and could go no further.

He clicked his tongue and whistled, beckoning. *All right, new plan.* Without a beat, I scurried down to the floor and made a break for the spiral staircase on the left. I looked up to the balcony to make sure I could find him amongst the stacks, but he darted into the dark where I knew he'd be waiting.

When I finally made it up, trying to rein in my panting breaths, the black monolithic shelves hid him well. My chest quaked, body tensed for the attack, smile unable to be pushed into a concentrated frown. I caught myself wondering why I was chasing a total stranger.

"Come on, Raggedy Andy . . ." I murmured, biting my lip as I slowly took in each corner.

I patted the bookcases as I passed them. Solid. Nothing hiding in them, behind them . . . safe. I cast my searching eyes just ahead and up. At the end of the aisle was a short staircase with a black door at the top. I fixated on it for a second, wondering if he could've sneaked away up there, but there was a rush of air on my right. Out and fast came Li, and I braced myself as he lifted me from behind, twirling me as I kicked the air midspin. His hands held fast and kept me airborne.

"Okay, okay!" On a reflex I kicked out, which made the up-til-then perfect performer catch his foot and bring us both down. We slammed tailbones-first into the hardwood. All I could do was laugh at the look of utter shame on Li's face at having made such a terrible landing. I was surprised that we were having fun, were laughing, were finding all this *acceptable*. Especially since I didn't know anything about this mystery boy.

I sat up and shuffled back-first into a shelf as he composed himself, but he got me by the ankle. He held out his hand, pointing to the camera, then flicking what was left of his photo pile. A trade.

I huffed. "Fine then."

The pictures and the camera changed hands, and we both weighed our prizes as equals.

"Agh." I scrunched my nose at one of my mug, captured midscreech. "Too much of a close-up."

He snagged the picture from me and held it up to my blinking face. He shrugged as if to say, *looks the same to me.*

I flicked that one at him. "Gee, thanks."

I dove back into perusing the stack at hand, until the camera flashed and I flinched away. "Okay, already! One's *enough*! What's so special about my face, anyway?"

Laughing in his almost noiseless way, he physically zoomed in for another take. The flash went off, but without result. His elation deflated as he shook the thing at his ear.

"It's out of *film*," I sang tauntingly, stealing the thing back before he could chuck it elsewhere. "I'll get more, don't cry about it."

After stowing the camera and the pictures safely in my bag, I turned to see that Li had adopted his never-ending stare tactic again, blinking and expectant, eyes boring deep into me like twin mining drills. I pushed a stray bit of hair behind my ear, trying to ignore how my face was getting hot, and looked down.

"Look, I . . . I'm really grateful for yesterday, you know. You were gone before I could *really* thank you, so I'm glad you're here again and that I could say thank you properly . . . even though you're sort of a scary kleptomaniac, but I don't mind, really, there are weirder things to be . . . but yeah, I just wanted to say thanks, and I'm also glad you're here, because there are a few things that have been bugging me about this place, about yesterday, the whole thing with my hand . . . and how you got in here, too—"

When I looked back up he was closer than before, still staring, and I reflexively nudged him on the shoulder to get the message across; if he moved any closer I'd be impaled on his angled nose.

"You've gotta stop that," I said, standing my ground. "You don't have to keep staring. If there's something you wanna say, just say it."

Parting his hair from his eyes, Li looked away, ashamed, crossing his legs and folding his hands in his lap. I waited for him to say something, anything, and just as I was about to lay into him for ignoring me, for playing this terrible game with me that wasn't funny anymore, I saw what little colour he had was draining from his cheeks. He put a slender-fingered hand around his neck, looked me straight in the eye, and shook his head. A breath hissed and caught in my throat as it thickened.

"Oh," I said, sounding just as dumb as I felt. "Oh. I'm so sorry. I just thought you . . . I don't know *what* I thought, I guess." *Mute-button eternal. Maybe* you *should practice that every once in a while, Ash . . .*

Li waved his hands, trying to make it seem like it really wasn't that big a deal. He patted me on the shoulder, reached over, and picked up half of my pile so he could have a good look, too. We sat in the musty quiet, all the hundreds of questions I had suddenly seeming pretty mediocre and small. I felt like I had no right to talk, worried and embarrassed that it would make Li feel bad. He nudged me in the ribs, probably sensing this, trying to get me to lighten up. I scooped up a Polaroid.

"This one's my favourite so far," I said, handing over a close-up of the deer clock. "I wish you hadn't wasted all that film. I don't have a proper one of you, but hundreds of me."

He made a noise like *tsk*, rolling his eyes. The pictures were my proof. Maybe I needed proof that he was real, too. At least today he looked more apt to play, happier, lit up from the inside, even. My mind kept flashing between the relaxed smile of now to the drawn and worried grimace of then. Was he here hiding from something? Or someone . . .

Tabitha. I fumbled through my bag for my cell, checking

the time. Two missed alerts. *Damn, I was supposed to be over there half an hour ago.*

"Oh, God, sorry. I have to go." I scrambled to my feet. The library was meant to be my apology card, and all the proof of it, too. It had been my bright idea to document everything I could, then flash it at her as a means of bandaging over our sour parting yesterday. But as soon as I had slipped in here, my intentions fell away behind me.

Li got up just as fast, and as I was shouldering my bag and making my way to go, he was in my path. "I really have to go," I tried, ducking around him. I couldn't play with him forever, even though, I thought suddenly, I'd like to.

He grabbed me by the bag but I yanked free, serving him a triumphant raspberry as I bounded off.

"You're holding me up, crazy boy," I shouted, words ricocheting here and there off shelves and balcony rails as I skipped down the stairs. "We'll talk more again, sometime . . . Well, *I'll* talk more, right?"

I looked up at the railing where Li had followed as far as the landing would allow, stopping at the edge restlessly. I genuinely thought he was going to try to swan dive after me, his confident trickster mask cracking free. *Will I see you again?* his apprehension whispered.

I tried to offer a flimsy buffer of comfort, because I felt he deserved it. "I'll come back soon. We seem to like the same haunts. I'm sure we'll see each other again."

His eyes darted around the room, frustrated. He was searching for words without sound, so he plucked them from the air with his fingers. Point to me, point to him, panoramic hand view.

"Me, you, here?" I translated. His nod was more than

eager, body dangerously pressed to the railing in order to be close without jumping down. I laughed and rocked on my heels. "What makes you think I spend my summers meeting crazy thief boys in abandoned libraries?"

Shrilling out a whistle, he twirled his finger at his temple and pointed at me.

"*I'm* the crazy one?"

Curt nod.

I couldn't help it. He was master and commander of an entire circus all on his own, and I didn't mind coming along for the tour. He was the colour and poetry that Treade owed me.

"All right!" I agreed. "When?"

He held out his hand, beckoning me for an offer.

"Tomorrow?" I laughed. "How about tomorrow?"

The corners of his lips twitched like nothing could make him happier. I had never felt so wanted with so few words to prove it, and it made my chest expand as I found my exit hole. Could there really be something *that* special about me? A candid thought reverberated sharply through me as I squeezed out into the open, trying to avoid clumps of mud and wall debris.

Li was just one more *last* to add to this summer's list.

· ○ ● ○ ●

I rounded Tabitha's downhill bay, trying to keep my knees in check on the slope so I wouldn't find myself with a mouthful of sidewalk. My sheer, brilliant excitement alone propelled me like a meteor. Two days had been enough time for me to keep all this a secret. Tabs had to know, had just as much right as me to know, and soon there would be no dissension, no hurt, only lasting memories.

And right after, we'd pass the story on to Paul, the words and inspiration slipping out of me like twinkling coins into his lap. Our reunion would electrify our tender souls back to life. The three of us would bask in this new adventure, this new sanctuary, relishing in the tale with each dive into it. After all the time we'd spent dreaming, the mystery would be ours. Our escape. Until time moved us on and tapped us out.

I came to the bottom of the bay hill, bag slapping feverishly against my back. The kingdom would be ours, and I had just the thing to get Tabitha back in on it.

My mind shunted so suddenly onto Li that it made me jerk to a stop just a house away from Tabitha's. His desperate, pleading eyes jutted out like chalk lines on asphalt, gemstones in the depths:

You, me, here?

He'd been in the library before me. The kingdom couldn't truly be mine, Tabitha's, or Paul's. Not really. Not with the brotherhood that Li's feet seemed to share with the floors and the walls, making him able to navigate the darkest shadow to save my sorry self. I had him to thank for letting me live to see this adventure come true. What would I tell them about Li, when I knew so little? Where did he go after I left? And had I ever seen him in town before? A population of under 3,000 made it hard to miss a face, but . . . there he was. At first he was so aloof and closed in, until he transformed into a wild mischief-maker needing chase and attention. So many fragmented aspects. Schizophrenic, joyful stranger — what could I expect from him? *Who* are *you, mystery boy?*

But his eyes, afraid of being lied to, afraid I would disappear in front of them. The teasing, the playing. It felt like this sharp expression of gratefulness for something I didn't know I had done. He was the one who had saved *me*, after all.

I'd promised Li I'd see him tomorrow. *I owe him more than I can imagine*, I suddenly realized. More than a promise, anyway. It hit me harder as I walked slower down the sidewalk, the enthusiasm draining into the cracks I stared at. I suddenly felt trapped between two worlds, unable to compromise or cultivate the promises I had made to either one.

Just him and me. How would he feel if the others were there? He could say nothing, his silence worse than words.

I woke up from all the thoughts shuddering behind my eyes like caged moths, and found myself on Tabitha's doorstep. My hand was poised on the knocker, even though I didn't even remember putting it there. I was so close, but the hesitation reel had caught into my skin and was pulling me back. I wanted to tell Tabs, I did, but a roughshod series of bad reasons made me drop my hand as I talked myself out of being accountable. I mean, to be fair, maybe her spark had gone out after all. If I gave her this last ember back, this little flicker, she'd expect more from me. So would Paul. Just as we were attempting the cut, we'd be freshly reattached at the hip. Maybe she was right. "You've let go, Ash, why can't we?" she had said, and the words assaulted me, even now. No, I decided. I couldn't tell her. My poor string of logic as to why I couldn't, though, was constructed by a careful, quiet shadow, one that wanted nothing and no one else to interfere with what it felt it had so long deserved. I wasn't willing to see that it was there, waiting in the pit of my stomach, so I let it have its way.

As I leaped off the doorstep and paced down the driveway, I suddenly felt like I was doing everyone a favour by keeping the secret close. That maybe it would be a better idea to share it later in the game, after I'd left, after the library was a blank slot in an empty town archive. I didn't want to disappoint anyone anymore, that was for sure, and I never wanted to see that look of absolute disenchantment on Tabitha's face again.

"Ash?"

End of the driveway, getaway averted, I jerked to a stop on one foot and pirouetted. There was Tabitha, door open, eyebrow cocked at me. In my blank surprise, I twitched out a smile.

"Hey, Tabs. Sorry — I, um. Didn't think you were home. No one answered when I knocked."

Liar.

She shut the door, barring the dog from leaping out behind her as she crossed the front garden and huffed a curl out of her eye.

"Didn't hear a knock," she said. "You could've texted."

Trapped. "Right. Well. I left my phone at home. Stupid."

Still lying.

We were silent, awkward. Then Tabitha blurted, "I'm sorry for yesterday, Ash. It's just . . . it's gonna be hard, you know, when you're gone. It's not because of—"

"No, no," I sighed, smiling, glad the ice was finally melting, "it's okay, Tabs. I understand. It's okay."

Looking away, eyes misty, she shrugged one shoulder and the subject dropped dead away into the concrete beneath our feet. I abandoned the stupid idea of not telling her about the library, my resolve cracking. I wanted to heal that heartbreak lining her face and wordless mouth. I pawed around in my bag for my pile of Polaroid Band-Aids — my own remedy for the soon-to-be wounds.

"Hey, I wanted to show you this," I said, fingers scrounging in excited plunges past my camera. They hit the bottom and found nothing else. I paused and kept looking, nearly putting my entire head in there, but my bag was empty, save one picture I looked at guardedly: the first photo I had taken of the library before going in. There was a fist around my heart.

Tabitha leaned in, speculating from her advantageous height. "Well? What is it?"

I couldn't decide if it was a blessing or not that the pictures had been stolen from me, yet again. Nervously, uncomfortably, I laughed a bit and shouldered the bag. "Damn. Must've left it at home. I have to go, though; didn't tell Mum I was going out. She's been having crazy mood swings with the move so close. She'll flip, you know?"

Tabitha's disappointment was palpable, but her confusion surmounted it. "You came all the way over here, though. Are you sure you can't just tell me what it is?"

I was already taking painful steps to leave her driveway. "No, no. I want to show you first. Anyway! I promise I'll show you tomorrow."

She just shrugged and came down off the steps to bundle me into a hug before I bounced away with a wave. We'd reconciled halfway. That was better than nothing.

"Bye, Tabs!"

As I curved round the corner, out of Tabitha's view, my eyes winced shut and I squeezed my arms around myself. In a kinetic mind flash I could see, could *feel*, Li grappling with my bag to keep me back in the library. My imagination made up for the interlude where I wasn't looking at him, and he must've grabbed the picture pile. I had felt them in my hand. I had taken them. They were solid. I opened my eyes and looked at said hand, the one that had met with so much trouble still disturbingly uninjured.

As I walked carefully home, shaking my head and feeling a bad, unfamiliar buzz coursing at my temples, I could clearly picture Li lounging in solitude in the quiet shadow of a book-case, poring contentedly through my pictures. And I was left empty-handed, with one Polaroid that meant nothing at all.

Nothing to anyone, except me.

She has made the best out of what little she had available to her on such short notice. The town hall sparkles with a hundred frosted lights, and the serving men are sharper than diamonds in their smooth tails. All locals, of course, but they enjoy playing the part, hustling martinis and canapés as though it were just another day on the grain line. And besides, they want to feel the light coming off him when he makes his toast.

The Fort Garry Hotel would have been a more suitable venue, she muses from the top of her champagne glass, the bubbles prickling her upper lip. But Treade has come through for her, yet again, just as she knew it would. She surveys the burgeoning party from a shaded alcove, greeting businessmen and their spouses with utmost courtesy, fawning over their attire — which has either come from the States or straight from the Hudson's Bay catalogue, but at least they've made a sporting go of it. Tuxedos and gowns, the upper crust of Winnipeg, having flocked to farm country for a mere birthday party, coo over the long ride in and just how *endearing* this little hamlet is. She can very clearly picture David's restless ghost scowling at the entire affair, drowning his contagious misery in gin. But not tonight. This is not his night, or his place anymore. She finishes the champagne and shudders, exhausted already.

"Shall I get you another, Mrs. Jovan?"

And there he is at her shoulder, sly and quiet, and just as apt as her to hide from the smattering of guests and attention. Like mother like son, as ever. They retire to the mezzanine for some privacy. He passes her another full champagne flute from a proffered serving tray along the way.

"You know," she says to him, "it is *your* birthday. Surely you could thank your friends for coming." She doesn't scold him, not truly. How can she, when she was avoiding the lot of them, too?

He looks heavenward as she puts the drink aside to adjust his silk tie. "They were my father's friends. Not mine. Neither of us have use for these kinds of things. They were always his affair."

"*He* cannot direct a burgeoning agribusiness from his grave, dear. And if you want this grain elevator expansion project of yours to succeed in Treade, you must woo the investors. If you didn't already know, our money is really theirs."

Reclaiming his tie, he eases his hand onto a coffee table covered in fresh gardenias behind him. They were no Broadway Florists' work, but as he fidgets with the petals, she sees none of it really matters anyway. He has been sulky since she declared his twentieth to be marked by such an elaborate occasion, and that his taking the mantle of Jovan Grain, his father's jilted legacy, was something to celebrate. Tonight it would be official, but he had been holding back from it. And she had known why. But she had not wanted to test the waters of it.

"I know you didn't want this. I know but . . . believe me, you *will* show all of those empty-headed socialites that their trust in you is not in vain." She takes his hand in her opera-gloved one. "I know you can do this. You have his charm, Nel. And his strength. Even though you did not see much of those traits by the end of it, they were there."

"That's enough," he forces through a smile. "Let's not talk about that. Tonight is supposed to be a celebration."

She steps back. Inspecting her reflection in the golden drink at hand, she snorts. "I believe that is my line."

Before she can register, he has taken the glass from her and downed the contents.

"Please don't," she grimaces.

A waiter has somehow found them, and he is already gone to fetch back a whisky. "Liquid courage," he shrugs.

Her eyes narrow. "I said channel his charm, not *become* him."

But that breaks him.

"I said *that's enough!*" The champagne flute shatters on the marble tile, and she recoils, speechless and shaking.

He is still, covering his mouth with a palm, before trying to smooth back his usually unruly hair, tidied tonight by enough pomade to sink a ship. His eyes soften immediately as she turns away, hand clutching the silk organza at her frail chest. She is bundled into his arms, and she does not fight as he leads her to a chaise, kneeling and taking her small hands in his. Acknowledging this weakness makes her even sicker than she already is.

"I'm sorry, Mama, I'm sorry," he whispers as he strokes her fine hair, hair that barely remembers what colour it may have been when she had been a girl, easily seduced by the uptown galas and the chance to swan endlessly around in a sea of champagne and frivolous lives. The cold, endless prairie may not have been Toronto or New York, but it offered delicate dreams in a harsh landscape. And she has smothered them all.

He looks at her earnestly. "I don't want his charm or his strength," he says. "They failed him when it was most important. I don't want any of him. Please. All we need is each other and this beloved town, not this business, this curse. Let us be rid of it. Let it be someone else's burden."

There it is, the dark thing that has hung between them since they arrived, and maybe even through all the years she had urged him through a business degree in preparation for this day. But without the business, there would be nothing for him once she was gone. Their name, their very claim to the upper society that had wrecked them, would fade in the annals of an already subpar province. She wanted it all; the magic that this town had worked on their ruined family, and the tremendous boons that marrying an alcoholic agribusiness monarch had given them. But her son has never wanted that. He yearns for the simple life that this farm town has offered, for the solitude of his books, for the peace that grounds him firmly in place. But with Jovan Grain, they could have every dream they grasped for. She could not let him abandon that now. Not after all this time, when it's already too late.

She is smiling now, smiling as if someone has only just asked her, *Isn't the night divine?*

"You should prepare your toast, love," she says, patting his face. "Everything will be fine. *I'm* fine. After tonight, we can talk about anything you like, all right? We will be set after the ghastly affair is done with. You'll see."

Worn down, he gets to his feet. His whisky arrives, and he swallows that, too, in one mean gulp. He beckons the server to leave him the still-full bottle, and he refills his mickey. His eyes are growing darker and darker, but she feels just as feeble watching him drown in this way, as she had been with her husband so long ago. She looks from the champagne flute shards on the floor to her poor son, and feels whatever fight she has left in her drain away.

"Would you like me to help you get some air?" he offers, but she waves him off.

"Don't worry about me. Go, enjoy the party. It's your night."

Adjusting his jacket, he has not even the energy to fake a smile. She has hurt him with this, all of this. "I think *I* will get some air, then," he says, bending down and kissing her on the cheek. His frustration is carved in his slumped shoulders, as he gets farther away from her, his gait an exaggerated attempt at keeping from stumbling.

She whispers "Happy birthday," but he is gone. This is the last time she will ever see him.

DATE
ISSUED TO
CHAPTER SEVEN
PROPERTY OF
TREADE
PUBLIC LIBRARY

In the dream, this time, I am down deep in the water. I know it is Lake Jovan, can tell by how green the water is, how murky, the lake weed choking the bottom like angry cilia, loose garbage stuck in an eternal tableau in the depths. Even in the dream I think this isn't unusual.

But there is something else, other shadows tumbling through the black surface of the lake above my head. I swim closer, twisting, reaching out. The shapes clarify; they are books, pages coming loose like soggy flesh in my hands. I let them sink behind me into nothing. I swim and I swim, and the farther I go, the thicker the water becomes with books. Pretty soon, with every stroke of my arms, I am hitting them on all sides. The water is being displaced, and I am being drowned by them.

There is someone else with me. I know it before I see her. She is floating in the book mire, and I nearly crash straight into her. She isn't moving, floating there as lifeless as the water, the lake weed, the books. She is as much a part of the lake as they are. And she has endless hair, white, milky, and it blurs her face from me. I stick my hand in and try parting it so I can see her, because I feel I'd know her, and I need to know for sure.

Her eyes snap open as soon as I am able to get a good look at them. Then her hands go for my throat, and she drags me to the bottom.

· ∘ ● ∘ ●

I woke up on the floor, tangled in my bedsheets. I'd knocked over one of the many stacks of books I had on the nearby floor and the bedside table, too. My neck was sore from having used a few of them as pillows during the night in my sleep. I had no idea how long I'd been down here. I had never fallen out of bed before.

I tossed everything back in its place and looked out the window, pushing my dancing princess painting to the side. In the immediate distance was a grain elevator, an enormous J inside a diamond painted on the whitewashed brick. "J for Jerktown," Tabitha had said once, in one of her more bitter moments. The elevator had always been there, blocking out the sun as it set every single day for ten years of my life. When we first moved here, I had told Mum that it must be Rapunzel's tower, and one day it would be mine, too. She just smiled and let me dream.

Those elevators were sprinkled all over Manitoba, though, appearing on postcards and sometimes in our textbooks at school. The J itself had become a sort of provincial staple, and Treade was proud, to some extent, to boast two or three of them. The history behind the elevators and the people who owned them had faded now, the story of it on some plaque yet to be set up. But with the ethanol plant providing most of the town's income, Treade had little use for the abandoned grain towers and all they implied. As usual.

The house was empty, the sun shone on my Rapunzel elevator, and my heart was raring to go. There was no time like the present to fulfil my promise. Before I could exhale, I was darting through the suburbs and open fields, getting lost in my head.

I found myself standing in front of the Fable Door so quickly that the effort it took to get here seemed like it had happened to someone else. I fingered the carvings, which always looked like they were submerged in the wood, diving through the waves on their way to worlds elsewhere. I had this urge to fling the door open and walk in through the front, bold as brass, taking ownership of the place like it was mine instead of having to scurry in the back way like a squirrel seeking refuge. I tugged on the chains and, as usual, they wouldn't budge.

I spent some time clearing away my hole, making it easier on myself, and Li, too, to keep getting in and out. Now that I thought about it, this *had* to be how he'd been getting in here; probably saw me doing it on that rainy afternoon and followed me in like a shadow . . . even though he was so much taller than me, and it'd be a wonder to see him fit through at all. Short of him passing through the walls, though, there was no other way.

I pulled over an abandoned piece of rusted sheet metal from one of the various scrap piles leaning against the building, keeping it at the ready to cover my tracks when I left. I'd been pretty careless so far; if any of those new property owners showed up to appraise the place after that storm, they'd see my and the tree's handiwork faster than we'd made it. I didn't want to take the chance anymore. I crawled in.

Morning sun filtered through the rose window, tinting the library in the pinks of the glass. I shut my eyes and inhaled; the old book smell was like a cake cooling on a windowsill. Potent. Inviting. I wanted to soak it up, and I twirled in the joy of it, dancing in the dust motes caught in the light, and revelling in the discovery of this sanctuary. A palace of books, of dreams themselves. My perception of the library had shifted in spite of (or because of) my misadventures here: I felt safe, felt at home, and calm, too, even though Li could pop out from any corner and catch me off guard. And even though I didn't know him at all, and that we especially didn't have much to talk about . . . I found myself missing him.

"Li?" My voice bounced off the books and vanished. I was probably early. But I was still excited. Maybe we shared more than I thought. Maybe he was the answer to all my empty hopes for this town. Maybe he was a dreamer that had been ill-treated by Treade, too.

Or maybe he just hung out here to get away from his overbearing parents.

Either way, there was something about him, the way his eyes barbed into me like they were willing me to keep still. How he flitted from one place to another like a handful of light. How he so badly wanted to see me again. Or had that just been a hopeful daydream, too?

Deciding to wander around while I waited, I wove from stack to stack. The books were endless, each one a speck in a universe. I wondered where they came from, where the covers had been bound, where the gold foil had been stamped. Some books were musty and worn, others looked unopened and fresh, and I could see that many were first editions. I snatched them up like precious stones, and after a handful of random selections, I settled in perfect quiet with Oscar Wilde in hand. There was a beautiful engraving of Dorian's portrait on the facing page, and I touched his brooding brow to feel the smooth parchment paper against my finger. It was so new, I could feel the grooves of where the press had insinuated the image.

That's when I heard the flapping.

It broke the silence so hard that I jumped, dropping the book. I stood still, thinking it was just another one of *his* tricks. "Li? Is that you?"

I scooped the book back up, trying to find the source of the noise, or at the very least detect Li's shadow nearby. But I was totally alone. I heard a rustling, and then again the flapping. It sounded like someone shuffling a newspaper restlessly, and it was getting closer.

I looked up and something white flashed above me, diving for my head with its wings spread. I ducked as it swooped back up and flocked to the banister of a nearby landing. I raced out to meet it, stopping short a few feet to get a good look at it. It was big, about the size of a crow, with an unforgiving beak. In the light it looked creamy beige instead of white, and it was speckled with indiscernible black markings.

"How did you get in here?" I wondered aloud. There might have been a hole in an eave somewhere; the place was old enough. But as I got a closer look, I realized that it was definitely not a bird I had ever seen on the prairie before, and as it preened under a wing and I squinted at it, I felt no closer to knowing. When I took one step too close, its head swivelled my way and it opened its beak. Not a sound came out, and before I could move, it had taken a direct dive for me and stolen the book from my hands in its outstretched talons. It vanished into the dark corners of the library.

"Well," I said, keeping the dialogue-with-no-one going, "okay, then."

Further rustling. But this time it was the sound of a page turning, and as I whipped around, there he was, clearer than the daylight dancing through the rose window.

"Oh, hi!" I said, breathless with enthusiasm.

He stood with his back to a bookshelf, the jacket I'd seen him wearing both times we'd crossed paths now slung over his shoulder, revealing a wrinkled — but pristinely white — button-up shirt that seemed like it belonged on Jay Gatsby and not this continuous trickster of mine. He was reading, and what I first took to be immersion in whatever the book was, turned out to be just another prank, as the book was upside down in his hands. He still didn't look up, though; didn't even seem to register that I was there.

I waved my hand in front of him. "Hellooo?" But as soon as I started waving, his hand lifted up to copy me. I stopped and lowered mine. So did he. He suddenly looked up from the book and at his hand, bewildered that it was moving of its own accord. We were suddenly trapped in a grainy Chaplin film.

I took a step back until the gulf of the aisle between the bookcase rows stood between us. He put the book down and backed up, too, never meeting my eyes. We judged each other, poker-faced and trying to predict the next move. I pinwheeled my arms gracefully in the air, one at a time before doing a slow twirl. He followed suit, trying to keep a very serious face as we performed these mock-ballet moves, shuffling our feet in complement. I lurched forwards suddenly and he caught on just in time. Danced to the left, now to the right. Twirling, arms up again, into the aisle, and out from the row.

We mirror kids were nearly nose to nose, hands up. Who was the original image now? Who called the shots?

We stood there in the silence for what seemed like a decade, daring each other to break the spell. Somewhere close by, I heard what had to be that bird flapping. I twisted away.

"Did you hear that?"

As usual, Li's way of replying was as far from words as he could get. He jumped out of our mirror dance and grabbed my hands, spinning the both of us in dizzy circles and distracting me from any noise, had there been one. I stumbled but he caught me, and we laughed as he helped steady me on my feet.

"You're crazy!" I puffed, far from being genuinely peeved as I gave him a playful nudge. He just smiled and looked down, collecting his jacket where it had fallen and draping it over a nearby chair. He looked a little sheepish.

"What, you didn't think I'd come back?" I teased. He shrugged, but his eyes shone with gratitude. "You must be really bored, hanging around an abandoned library just to mess with me."

He puffed out his cheeks and rolled his eyes, pivoting on a heel back towards the bookshelf. I followed as he plied a few books free, balancing them on his head, feet feeling for the invisible trapeze line.

"Really bored," I said, following him close and walking his line, "to take all my pictures just to make sure I came back." A surprised chuckle rose up as he lost one of his carefully balanced books to the floor. I rushed past him, snatching the last book from his head before he could get a hold of my shirt, and perched it on my head, instead.

"You know," I started, walking his trapeze backwards

now, "I don't think it'd be in my best interest to keep hanging around with a thief. Not good for my reputation, you know how it is." Hands clasped behind his back, his broad shoulders dipped down, he nodded and took on an air of gentlemanly understanding as he waltzed in my wake. I did a little twirl.

"And I really needed them, so that of course adds insult to injury," I pressed on, the book on my head wobbling a bit as my conviction started to slacken. He came around me in a slow half circle, appraising my form as he came to the other side, gently taking the book from my head. He clutched it to his chest like he was afraid it would get away, then revealed its cover and the title emblazoned on it in red cursive. He grinned like a clever cat. *Finders Keepers* by R. Stoat, it read. My mouth fell open and I just laughed. He gave a little bow and shelved it again.

"I would have come back anyway, you know," I said, flicking him hard on the shoulder. "When I make a promise, I keep it."

He beamed beatifically and pinched my nose before turning away, but I seemed to think there was something like relief in those grey eyes.

He darted towards another row, and I pursued, and though I tried to bound right behind him, he was gone.

"Aren't you *ever* going to stand still?" I crept alongside the bookcase with one hand on its contents to keep myself composed, until another hand shot out from an empty space between the books and made a grab for my wrist. I shrieked and evaded, backing into the case on the other side, but something was there to nudge me on the shoulder. It was the toe of a shoe, Li's shoe, and when I looked up, there he was, hanging idly off a sliding ladder.

"How did you do that?" I asked, bewildered by his sleight-of-everything.

He held up a finger as though he'd suddenly had an epiphany. He dug through his pockets, his sleeves, and only when he gave his curly head a scratch did it come to him. Reaching behind my ear, he thin-air snatched a Polaroid, tumbling it between his elongated, precise fingers. I took it before I could be teased with it, seeing that it was a picture of the deer clock on the back wall. A picture of time, a thing I was arrogantly convincing myself I had in infinite supply.

This time, the flapping got both of our attention. We both looked up, and floating down on us with all the grace it had failed to show before was the white bird. It kicked up its little feet before settling on Li's outstretched hand. I was delighted at first, thrilled and awed that I was going to be able to get up close, but my face fell. I backed away, and both Li and the bird looked at me as though I was the crazy one.

"What is that?" I pointed, feeling my spine tighten with something like shock. "How are you doing that?"

He and the bird tilted their heads in concert, absorbing my words as they both took a closer look at each other. The bird puffed itself up, each individual feather rustling in that familiar *papery* way. Because that's what the bird was made of. It did not have curves on it, but folds, and those black markings I couldn't make out before were letters, because the paper was book pages. I had searched Treade for some magic, and here it was, right in front of me. I just couldn't accept it.

Li jumped down from the ladder; the bird barely stirred. He came slowly towards me, his free hand reaching out and taking my wrist so he could position my arm properly. I let him mould me like an obedient marionette as he turned his own arm so it eased against mine, giving the bird an easier means to pass between us. Li's touch was so cold, but I stayed quiet, afraid that if I showed any real apprehension I'd lose the moment. A ripple of kinetic energy sizzled through my skin as his arm pressed into mine. I tensed, not knowing what to expect, but as the bird gingerly raised one talon, then the other, and settled on my wrist, I smiled. It didn't weigh anything; it was paper, after all. I experimented with moving my hand up and down, and though it shook its head and ruffled itself up again, it didn't fly away. I forgot that I had been afraid only a few seconds ago.

I looked up at Li, whose smile crinkled his eyes. "You really are a magician," I whispered. "How can you be doing this? It's like . . . breathing origami or something."

He ran a hand down the bird's breast affectionately, like they were old friends. It dipped its head down, gratefully. Lost in his thoughts, Li's face grew far away, going to a place that I couldn't see. I knew he couldn't answer in the way I was used to, so I tried to read him, tried to divine what was beneath the surface of his skin, but I got nowhere.

"Li?" I broke the silence. Suddenly, the bird on my hand collapsed, and I gasped, trying to catch it. It had quickly unfolded itself and reasserted into a pile of wrinkled pages at my feet. Li looked genuinely stricken. I stood there dumbly, bending down to pick the paper up, feeling like I had just broken all of the bird's fragile bones, if it had any. It had seemed so real in my hands.

"I . . ." I mouthed, trying to hand the pages back to him. "I'm so sorry. Can you . . . ?" *Can you fix it? Can you make it alive, again?* The questions sounded even stranger in my head.

All I could say was "I'm so sorry" again and again, unable

to control my irrational feelings of guilt over ruining something so precious and remarkable. His hands were instantly over mine as he shook his head. *It's all right*, his eyes softened. He guided me into the centre aisle, right into the light of the rose window, pages in hand.

He was clasping my hands tight, and this time I didn't try to get away or incite a chase. This wasn't part of his slapdash comedy routine or his one-boy-circus act. This was something sacred. He turned my palms up and put one of the pages into them, his other hand over my eyes. I shut them obediently.

"What are you—"

He shushed me with one finger to my mouth. I swallowed. Then, before I could guess what he was going to do, he rested his hand right over my sternum. My heart rose to the occasion and beat against it. Other than Paul, I'd never been this close to or alone with a boy, let alone someone like Li; someone who shone from their centre, someone who made even the air around him buzz with possibility — all without saying a word. These thoughts rushed through my head as he pressed in harder, like he was trying to knead my heart in his palm. I was about to tell him to stop, until I felt the paper in my hand twitch.

I opened my eyes because I had to see this. The corners of the page were curling up, edge by edge, as if it was looking for a good place to start its life. I stood very still, barely breathing, feeling my pulse in my temples as the page straightened itself in portrait right there in my hands. It seemed to shiver. Li was as focused on it as I was, and he reached out a long finger to gently poke the paper right in the middle. A ripple passed through it, and in its wake were the insinuations of fold lines. Our eyes darted together, and grinning, he quirked both eyebrows at me. *Go on*, they encouraged. I focused on the page, trying to summon everything whimsical in me that I could imagine, and with a rush in my heart, I gave the paper a poke.

Fold, tuck, pull, revolve. I suddenly had a paper sparrow pecking at my palms, looking for paper seeds.

Speechless, I raised my palms up, and the bird took off into the light.

In the halo of Li's Cheshire smirk, all I could say was, "This whole place is magic, isn't it?"

He rolled his eyes, grabbed my hand, and took me for a chase after the little bird. It soared into the light of the rose window, and we lost sight of it.

We jerked to a stop, Li pulling me behind a bookcase and looking around like someone was hot on our trail. He had plunged us back into another game, and I was more than willing to dive right there with him. We were crusading archaeologists, maybe, pursued in the jungle by poachers as we sought the rare Paper Bird, which needed our help to evade the poachers' nets. Pace by pace we kept to the shadows of the shelves, each corner holding the possibility of being discovered, framed, or betrayed. In a rush, he pointed. There was a flash of light, the sparrow hopped into view, then took off again. We stumbled after it, climbing the curving iron staircase right on its tail, and listened to our footsteps fall away like raindrops behind us.

Maybe it was seeing the bird come to life, maybe it was my willing heart, but for a moment I thought that the ground had some give to it, like the squish of wet, warm moss beneath my sneakers; thought I felt beads of sweat dot my neck, and that, in the distance, something exotic was *caw*ing across the infinite canopy. The library felt like it was fading around the edges, giving way to something else, *somewhere* else, but every time I tried to grasp it with my eyes, it became solid again. And Li was there right along with me, playing the stoic Indiana Jones type *en pointe*, never missing a beat. How could we be sharing the same daydream, connected by a slender thread in the midst of infinity?

Stepping carefully on the landing, Li suddenly stopped, swerving his head around. *We've been spotted*, said the sudden twitch at the corner of his mouth. And also, *we're doomed!* Someone had loosed a booby trap on us and there was little time to escape. Our only apparent salvation was at the top of those mysterious stairs I had seen yesterday, the door, now that I could see it closer, seemed to be made out of the wall itself. We heard a rumbling — or did we? — of falling rock, and though we were on the doorknob quick as anything, it was jammed. Li patted himself furiously for a key, gesturing wildly, feeling our end drawing near. I shook him, demanding he *snap out of it*, and just as we were about to be toast, a rustling of wings made us both look up. The bird pecked on the lintel, and the door swung inward.

We shut it behind us to keep any imaginary poacher or their offensive rock slide at bay, panting at the relief of our adventure marathon coming to a close. The game fell around our ankles and we looked at each other, laughing midcollapse and wondering what got into us. I don't bother asking what had happened, because I wasn't sure it had happened at all.

A light tapping drew my eye around the room. I followed it along, and there was the little sparrow, perched on the edge of a small porthole window near the ceiling.

I looked around for a stepstool, and when I came up with nothing, gestured at Li. "Hey, can you give me a boost?"

He picked me up like I weighed as much as the sparrow. I tried not to turn red or let my face get hot, because this is what friends did, boost each other up to windows . . . in magic libraries while you tried to catch a paper sparrow from flitting away. *Right.* I reached out to cup the little thing in my hands, but it hopped away, persistently tapping against the glass.

Out there was the library's back property, lined by Wilson's Woods and the other abandoned junk. It seemed so far away, like I was looking into a faded photo whose meaning had changed just as much as I had. I held on to that sensation, let this enchanted world I occupied be my home instead. Out there, the morning light struck the trees, especially the ones busted up by the storm, and transformed their broken bodies into something of a miracle. Something so destroyed made into something that could, at least, pretend to be alive in sunlight. I was torn, wanting to dart between those trees with Li as easily as we did through the shelves, and never wanting to have to cross those woods to go home again.

The sparrow and I regarded each other. We were on the same page. "I think he wants to be set free," I said, reaching for the rusted clasp that kept the window closed, the sparrow hopping excitedly at my hand. Li suddenly put me down.

"Hey!" I protested, but he leaned into me and scooped the bird out of the window. He carried it over to a fireplace, one big enough to stand inside, at the other end of the sitting room. He opened his hands there, and the bird fluttered up and away. I climbed into the fireplace from behind him; the walls were close for him, but nonetheless, I fit in there, with space enough to twirl.

This place really was a palace. "It's amazing! It's so big!" I peered into the shadows of the flue, and sure enough there was more fluttering. Little nests had been made in the incongruities of the brick, made out of shredded pages and anything else available. This was their aviary, and as I felt a hundred paper eyes settle on me, I decided not to disturb it any longer.

"I don't know if I can really trust my eyes, anymore," I said, absently running my hand along the carved mantelpiece, which was devoid of anything personal or revealing about this place — no photos, no mementos. But from the way the door had been deliberately painted into the wall, I could tell that this sitting room was to always be a secret, to be private. A retreat. There was a sofa in the middle, all red velvet and curved, looking like something out of Louis XIV's cat-scratch bedroom. Fit for a king, but whose throne could it be? And books in here, too, but no shelves; they were spread around the floor in piles, just like in my room, some full open like they had just been freshly read and abandoned, midsentence.

I picked across the glossy hardwood floor, trying to make my dirty shoes avoid the crimson and gold tasselled rug, whose woven patterns looked like a hundred stars all blossoming outward. Li had eased himself down by the sofa, pulling from his pocket one of the pages that used to be the crow-like bird I first saw. It floated in front of him and became a hummingbird, thought coalescing in form like mercury. I knelt down on the carpet at his feet, tucking my ankles under me as I watched the fragile creature flutter like a heartbeat in his hands.

"How can any of this be real?"

The hummingbird folded in on itself, midair, and the page that had just been alive floated quietly down to the sofa. Li glanced down at me, squinting, pointing at my heart and nodding, then pointing to my forehead and frowning.

I got it, easily enough. "Usually when someone says *trust your heart*, it means they don't have any clue what's going on either."

That got him. His smile broke against his mouth like a wave.

I guess I'd just have to accept it, paper birds, almost jungle, and all. But now that he was sitting still, I figured he would be willing to answer some more questions, in as much as he could in his own way. I got up and pulled him to his feet. "How long have you been coming here, Li?"

Eyes dropping to the ground, then swooping back up in the air, he seemed to be genuinely calculating. He drifted to a nearby wall, smoothing it out at first with one hand, then the other. He looked like he was feeling around for an answer, listening for something inside. But he came away without one, turned to face me, and stretched out his arms.

A long time.

"Really? Man . . . I'm jealous!" I threw my arms up, reaching out to mimic him and smooth out the cool plaster of the wall. "I would give anything to have found this place years ago." This place. This den of mysteries and enchantment. Where magic lay in concentrated wait before being snuffed out. It could have changed so much.

When I turned back to him, he was staring at me with those relentless, piercing spheres. He quickly looked away and shook his head, like I shouldn't really be jealous of him after all.

"It would've also been nice to have met you sooner, too," I dared to admit, pivoting towards him. "Have you lived in Treade for long? I've lived here forever and I've never seen you before. And believe me, I would have seen you." *I would have been drawn to you*, I thought, but I swallowed that away like a lot of my awkward adolescence.

He didn't look up or even try and sign an answer. "You *are* from Treade, aren't you? Or maybe Winnipeg? Do you have family here?"

Leaning the back of his head against the wall, he shut his eyes and let go of an immense sigh. He pointed to the floor.

"What?" I looked down. "You mean . . . here? You don't . . ."

Slowly, his eyes opened. A smile flickered past his teeth.

"Li . . . you *live* here?"

I'd never considered the idea until it had fallen out of my mouth. If I had asked myself before, I wouldn't have believed my head. But his way with this room, the mischief in his eyes . . . the library's blueprints were his fingerprints. It was more his mansion palace than it would ever be mine, and he was the vagabond king.

Some of his vitality came back, my moment of realization floating off towards the climbing sun as he took credit for my guess. He curtsied, welcoming me into his sacred inner sanctum. I returned the favour.

"Well, thank you for having me, and for not kicking me out when you had the chance." I laughed. "I hope you don't get in trouble for squatting here. You'll eventually have to hightail it once they tear this place down though . . ."

He cocked his head, unsure of what I meant. "Well, some development company owns this place, now. That's okay. You really don't have to stay here, though. Really. Whatever the problem is, you can always come to my mom's place. We have a spare room and—"

Even as I offered, I knew it wouldn't fly. He waved me off like I was one of his court jesters who was offering too many empty praises to the king. I wondered what Mum would think if I brought a strange, homeless mute boy home, especially one that dressed in the wrinkled remains of a suit shirt and pants, with eyes like gleaming agate who could do real magic. Bend reality. Make true dreams. She probably wouldn't think much of it, anyway. But Li was as hard to pin down as the little bit of light filtering through that porthole window. And that just made me want to see him more often. Keep him company. Harmonize the threads of our daydreams. Even if, for a second, I wondered if it was something sinister that had forced him to hide here. I shook my head.

"Okay, fine, I'll let you continue being homeless and I won't say a word to anyone. That's your business." I acquiesced and bowed low, and he knighted me with an invisible sword, welcoming me into his fold. "Besides, who wouldn't want to live in a library?"

DATE
ISSUED TO
CHAPTER SEVEN
CHAPTER EIGHT
PROPERTY OF
TREADE
PUBLIC LIBRARY

I have always had books. I couldn't remember ever being without them. In them was the magic the world was all too keen on forgetting. Every moment of my life could have been a line, every shining memory an etching beside a chapter heading. I always had two books on me — just in case I finished one, I'd always have a backup. Books were my way of losing myself, of dreaming myself elsewhere and elsewhen. Every single one became my world in the reading, while the real world turned, ignored, under my feet.

When I was twelve, I was in love with Jake Ackerman. He wasn't anything special, and he'd never said a word to me, but my daydreaming made him into someone else. He was from the upper school of Treade Collegiate, and I sometimes saw him reading at lunch period . . . when he wasn't surrounded by his goofball buddies, anyway. But he had a golden mane like Aslan, held himself like Holden Caulfield without the entitlement, and had the kind of eyes that might have (wrongly) convinced Catherine that Heathcliff was not the devil incarnate after all. He was also on the junior high football team, and I was obsessed with romance and the concept of true love happening anywhere, anytime. Always hopeful, in an awkward kind of way. But the awkward ones were always dreaming their way out, and I was keen to do the same.

So I went to all his games, which were always losing ones. I'd sit at the top of the bleachers, bent over a book, only looking up when Jake's number forty-two flashed feebly across the field. And one day it flashed my way.

"Hey, it's the *reader*," one of the guys with him said, passing my bleacher on their way home after the game.

"Yeah," I shrugged, putting my *Secret Garden* face down in my lap as all his friends looked on, shoving each other and grinning as my face grew hotter. I looked quickly at Jake.

One of the boys snorted, "Aww, I think she likes you, Jakey. Jakey loves to read all kindsa girly shit, too, dontcha buddy?"

This was his chance to come to my rescue, that John Hughes moment where he told them all to back off and admitted that we were made for each other. Our eyes met. His Heathcliff eyes crinkled in disgust like someone had barfed at his feet. Then he looked away. "You guys wanna go to 7-Eleven or not?"

They continued down the end of the field like I hadn't been there at all. And I wish I hadn't.

But now . . . I sat on the vanity stool in my bedroom, contemplating my face in my chipped-plaster mirror as all the Jake Ackermans in my life slipped away like old skin. I had no use for them. The stories I read, those fantasies and adventures. They were my swords in the dark. They were what kept me from giving up on myself, on my heart. They were woven into the fabric of me, and I did not need to be rescued by anyone. I would be the hero of my fairy tale, real or not.

Except now I was inhabiting that fairy tale in a way I never thought possible.

The magic of it, the library, Li. All of it rolled together in my chest and became my secret. And maybe I was Li's secret, too. But he took ownership of it, let it infiltrate his flesh and blood and become part of him. It was happening to me, too, because this secret was shaping me, insinuating folds and creases where there were none, and throwing me into the air like a paper bird. I twitched a smile at myself in the mirror, and a gentle hum revved up beneath my breast bone. There was magic in this world to be grasped at, and I was a part of it. My eyes darted to the porcelain masks and china jesters hanging drolly about the mirror, trappings I'd collected over the years because I somehow thought they'd bring me closer to Wonderland, to Oz. But I'd found it without them; it was *me* that made that sparrow fly. It was in me, all along, in some way. And the library was where that power could grow. We spent the entire day wrapped up in paper charms, making hundreds of birds flit around us until the air was thick with them. I had touched them, felt them, seen them. And for now, that was enough for me.

The sense of possession I immediately felt was enough to make my nerves tighten, make my arms quake, and make my self-importance soar. Finally, something existed just for me in this sterile town where everything was everyone's until it was smothered. I alone was illuminated against the secret's quiet glow.

I padded kitten quiet down the stairs and into the kitchen, hopping and skipping over the tumult of boxes littering the floor that were, as yet, unfilled. Mum was already trying to square our lives away in a few cardboard cubes so we could start it anew somewhere else, but for the moment she had given up. I couldn't hear her puttering anywhere in the house, and, assuming she still hadn't come home from the night shift, I eased up my air of inconspicuousness. The night before, I had filled an old picnic basket with things she wouldn't miss: extra cheese, soup, canned veggies, sandwiches, fruit. Apple turnovers (store bought) and soda. As much as I could grab without it looking like we'd been raided. I didn't know where Li was getting food, or how, but I felt like I had to pay him back for giving me . . . well, something I couldn't explain yet. I must have got carried away in my giddiness to make good my escape, but facing my mother's appearance in the living room, I was graceful enough to give away only surprise. Instead of the usual curiosity, she smiled, kissed me on the forehead, and said, "Have a good time, sweetie."

I blinked as she climbed to the top floor, her slipper-shuffling and ensuing cigarette smoke fading to her room. *That was easier than I thought . . . Though,* I continued to reason in my head as I thrust the door open, *she probably just thinks that I'm heading out to see—*

As Paul shifted his Buick into park and Tabitha popped the passenger door, I saw why Mum had been so blasé.

I froze, feeling like my blood was draining out of my feet and onto our front stoop. Both guilt and bitterness reared their heads, battling for the victor in the pit of my stomach. My weakened smile at their approach raised the flag for bitterness's take of the win.

"What are you guys doing here?" I asked, letting the genuine shock play the part for me.

"Thought we'd drop by." Paul shrugged, passing a secluded glance to Tabitha. *Just like before.* Something else, something

I had not really taken account of in a few days, snarled to life inside my chest. How could it be jealousy when I'd been consciously avoiding them?

His plotting eyes targeted my basket. "Hey, picnic!"

"Yeah, I was . . ." If I said *meeting someone* the jig would be up. It felt like there really was a rock slide coming for me, but it was made out of empty excuses and awkward pauses, and there was no jungle or adventure waiting for me in the back seat of that car.

Paul took a step back, starting to appraise the truth. It was his turn to look hurt. "Well, if you're . . . busy . . ."

"No!" I scrambled to evade the truth. "I was . . . going to surprise Tabs." I looked at her and forced myself to nod. "Surprise."

Tabitha bundled me into a hug, laughing. I avoided her eyes. "We should go to the park," she suggested as they steered me towards the car. I had nothing left in my arsenal except weak compliance.

. ○ ● ○ ●

I kept checking my phone for the time from the confidence of my pocket. I had expressly promised Li that I would meet him at the library two hours ago. I sat in the park while Paul and Tabitha chatted on and on, knees brought up to my mouth as I watched Wilson's Woods beyond the baseball diamond, trying to send my thoughts there.

"Are you okay, Ash?"

I whipped my head in Tabitha's direction. "Oh yeah. Why?"

I loved them. I did. And I knew that, after this summer had turned away from us, there would be a lonely hole inside of me that they used to occupy. But for now, I drowned in the highly pressurized depths of my thanklessness, feeling every bit intruded upon as they tried to keep me involved in the conversation.

Tabitha crumpled the wrapper of a turnover and tucked it back into the basket. "Canned veggies? What, were you running away?"

I felt the corner of my eye twitch as I looked away again, aggravation stabbing at me when I realized they had raided my carefully packed food. "I guess I haven't packed a picnic in a while."

"Oh, hey, did you ever find that thing you wanted to show me?"

I clenched the sleeve of my shirt. "Hm? What?"

"The other day, you came by my place. What was it?"

I clenched harder, searching the inside of my eyelids for a lie. "Oh. No. I lost it. It was nothing. Just a . . . picture of something."

The wind screamed in high reprieve at any unyielding suspect on the ground. It was a terrible day to be outside in the open, but we were pacifying nostalgia, bad weather or not. I had even spent a little extra time doing my hair, feeling more girly than I ever had, because for the first time I had someone special waiting for me and only me. The wind had ruined that now, flattening it against my head like a veil, eroding me down to the core.

The more they talked, the more it felt like there was water rushing in my ears, like something solid was growing and separating us, making me deaf to them. I let the water rise, because the day had been stolen from me, and they were being greedy with my time when I wanted to invest it somewhere else. With *someone* else. If Tabitha had just gone with me a few days ago instead of shutting me out, they could have been a part of it, too. But right at that moment, I didn't want them to be a part of anything. Especially the library. Especially Li.

When I didn't laugh or add anything to whatever jokes the two delivered, Tabitha pinched my knee.

"What?" I snapped back, the offender recoiling once I'd barked her away. The two exchanged glances, and the beast inside snarled again with reproach for their misplaced judgement.

"You seem kinda out of it, Ash."

Paul's concern probed into me, his logic train building the rails as it moved. I bit the tongue that twisted inside my mouth as I shook my head, tempted to let it untangle and wag him into silence.

Tabitha nailed me deeper. "If it's about the other day, about our place . . ."

I got to my feet then, stretching with feigned casualness. I pocketed one hand and checked my phone, eyes blazing again at the lost time. I nabbed the basket and shrugged.

"It's kind of cold out here, and—" I managed a well-placed pause, all the possible excuses I could make bobbing to the surface of my impatience like shined apples. I plucked one, admiring its shine. "My mom needs a hand with squaring some stuff away that we had in storage. For the move, and all."

Not only was it convincing, but it cut them, too, reminding them that I had things to do in order to secure my getaway. We made our goodbyes with weakened hugs and hushed waves, and I granted myself the pleasure of jogging off. Before I got very far Paul stopped me, and I could barely rein in my contempt any longer.

"Want a ride home?"

I kept walking, waving him off, not wanting to waste any more time. "It's okay. You guys hang here. Don't let me ruin the fun."

I galloped down the hill past the playground, and at its end I turned, ducking down in a thick of trees. I felt instantly ashamed that I should hide from them now, waiting for them to pick up and leave so that I could prevent their attempt at being good to me. *You made a promise*, that dark beastie in my chest reassured me. I forgot that I had made my friends all kinds of promises, too.

Finally, after ten minutes that passed like snails caught in a glue spill, the two stood up and strolled down the field towards the road that would take them back to Paul's car. A smile shot up onto my lips like a triumphant arrow, ignoring the almost sad slump in my friends' shoulders as they ambled off, defeated. I was too caught up to notice I had done anything wrong as I sprung from hiding and headed for the chain-link fence.

· ◦ ● ◦ ●

I pushed the basket in before me as I crawled out from under the table, my eyes taking their sweet time, as usual, to adjust to the yellow light of the library. I rubbed them and looked around, trying to find where I'd put my basket. It had been at my feet only a few seconds ago, but things going helter-skelter around here really didn't surprise me as much as it should have.

"Li? I'm here! Sorry I'm late . . ."

I waited to hear pages turning, feet shuffling, even a book being shut. But there was a kind of silence now that I couldn't avoid. No paper wings, either, even for having made so many yesterday. Instead, the floor was amply strewn with scattered pages, hundreds of them, and not one of them was talking.

Something dripped onto my head, and I jerked up to find the source. Water, leaking in a steady rivulet from the ceiling, or somewhere high up, anyway, as far as I could tell. It hadn't rained in days . . . but that didn't stop the dripping from becoming more insistent, the *plik plik plik* against the hardwood tapping out a distress signal. After nearly taking a spill forwards, I registered a puddle pooling at my feet, and following it up a ways, saw the source coming from between some books on the shelves in the wall.

Whatever this water was, I didn't think it could be natural. Something was wrong.

"Li, I need to talk to you." I rounded the stacks and came back out towards my exit, and found him sitting on the long end table, clutching my picnic basket to his chest. His eyes looked small. And betrayed.

"There you are!" Those hurt eyes swivelled up to mine, levelling me, like I had no right to say anything. "I'm sorry I'm late, Li. I *am*! I was . . . held up."

He clutched the basket tighter, the wind from outside screaming against the library's walls, roiling in through my porthole and stirring the abandoned book pages into a dervish.

"Come on," I tried, thinking maybe this was a game. "I told you I would come, and I did. Just like last time, okay? Do you want to go outside for a bit? I brought you something . . ."

I reached out but his body stiffened. In my periphery, I saw those single offending drips grow and multiply, the puddle reaching nearly to my feet. The dripping grew into a steady rush on all sides, climbing down the walls and through the shelves like a silent fountain. The library was losing its clarity again, but this time it was more powerful. The lights flickered and buzzed, the wood creaking and swelling as it absorbed the water, and Li's eyes grew darker.

I looked around, bodily chilled at the scene that was unfolding around me. "Li . . . what's happening?" Whatever was going on here, it seemed to be because of him. Or because of me. *He thought I wasn't coming back.*

I climbed onto the table next to him, carefully prying the basket from his hands so I could take them in mine. They were freezing. I did my best to look straight at him, ignoring that the water had nearly reached the table. "C'mon, Li. How could I forget about you?"

He finally looked up. The lights settled into themselves again, and the creaking stopped. The water receded when he registered me there, holding his hands, blinking like he had been in the middle of a nightmare. I smiled.

"Look." I swung my legs from the table, landing on the floor that was now completely dry. I opened the basket and invited him to see. "I brought you something! Sorry, there was more earlier."

He reached out, but I snapped the lid closed. "Ah ah! Not until you cheer up a bit."

Slowly, surely, his lips spread into a smile and his eyes crinkled. He had been remembered and, because of that, restored. I could feel the air between us warming, the light of the library radiating brighter.

Li shook his tangled curls, and in one swift leap, he was on his feet, twitching and spinning off the table, slipping the basket onto his wrist as he waltzed me out of the corner.

He dipped me. "Okay, okay!" I protested, giggling. He

pulled me back up so our faces were close, but he put up a Polaroid barrier before it could get serious. This time, it was a picture of the winding staircase, notions and whispers hidden in the shadows where the flash could not reach. He waved it in a hypnotising metronome cadence, back and forth, then flipped it into the air. When it came back down, it was a goliath moth, settling on my fingertips.

"Wow," I sighed. Its leaf-shaped antennae twitched towards the sound of distant flapping, then it rose and drifted off to a lamp, while a small cloud of paper sparrows broke past the rose window and towards another shadow.

The birds had perched themselves all over, some more keen to investigate me than the other way around. Li flaunted down to the middle of the room, bouncing from chair to chair and onto one of the big main reading tables as he swung the basket up under his nose, ploughing through his trappings. His eyes lit up as he took out an apple turnover, holding it under his nose and breathing it in. He dropped the basket absently, admiring instead the pastry's dimensions and sensuality rather than eating it. I kept to the edge of the table, leaning my face onto my fists as I watched him pocket the turnover sacredly, as if eating it would lessen its value. His gratefulness was palpable as he bent, a gentle hand touching my head with affection.

I half-blushed, musing out loud, "What *is* the way to your heart, then?"

He winked, tapping his nose as though such a thing at this junction should be obvious. He shuffled his feet, doing a little twist, and kicked over a pile of books that had been sitting on the table. Toeing one up in the air like a hacky sack, he sent it soaring my way, and I had to clamber in order to catch it. It was navy blue and leather-bound, the cover bearing gold foil filigree and latticework, but no title. The spine read *Women of the Classics*. The book must have been at least sixty years old, and I held it reverently as I passed the pages under my fingers.

Li crouched down at my shoulder, eyebrows waggling in their urging way.

"What do you want me to—"

He scuttled closer, his head coming right to my shoulder as his hands reached around mine, thumbing the pages for me. Faint bristles at his jaw rubbed against mine. I held my breath, thoughts tangled up like they usually became whenever he got close to me. *There.* His finger tapped against a new chapter, the facing page a portrait of Helen of Troy. She was a soft, long-necked goddess, pensive and fair, stepping forwards when she should have stepped back. Her eyes misunderstood what was real and what could not have been.

Li's well-boned hands drew away, the tops of mine suddenly missing the touch. I shoulder checked after him; he'd settled back on his hands, relaxed and waiting. I blinked. He waved me on, pointing and pointing. *Go on*, he urged. *Read!*

"Okay." I cleared my throat.

My voice filled the room as I read of Helen's tragedy and betrayal. Helen argued with Aphrodite after finding Paris at her table. The goddess had entwined the two, but Helen rallied against it. But no mortal can protest the will of the gods. So Aphrodite erased Helen's past, and Helen lost herself to another world. Paris met her, and she, probably trying to claw out of the deception placed over her like a veil, let him take her "twixt the lily and the rose."

I raised my head from the page. The library had melted away, vanished, and there was, very clearly, a night sky above us. It was a colour that I couldn't pinpoint, torchlight fighting for focus against the stars. I was standing in the middle of a road made of individual stones and painted with peonies, olive trees dancing in the lilting breeze, and the night was hot against my cheeks. I plucked a flower petal from my hair, and it dissolved. Li was standing there with me, plucking a bloom from a nearby tree, and he slid it into the book, beside the portrait of Helen. He closed the covers.

I scarcely breathed, watching as the clay buildings, the stone road, the flowers, and the trees rippled and moved backwards, melting into the ground and dissolving in a quiet whirlpool. The shelves reconstituted, the floors reassembled. We were inside a Rubik's cube, watching the pieces click back into reality.

Li just smiled at me, taking the book out of my trembling hands and replacing it with another one. His hands enclosed mine. *Go on,* they said. *Read.*

This was just the beginning.

· ○ ● ○ ●

My fingers traced the lines and details of my painted, defiant princess, her face refusing to keep promises or secrets. I went back over her pigments like someone retracing steps that have led them to a deep and unknown country, marvelling at how little it took to get them lost. The shades and hues of the paint built my princess's figure, set her a course, and promised her a future. I decided I would be her Aphrodite and define for her the duty she owed her maker.

I twisted the easel around to reveal the canvas's backside hollow, tucking in the two Polaroids that Li had returned to me, the first pieces of my secret collage. It was surreal just to look at the pictures, the clock and the stairs, and feel relieved that the photos, at least, could exist in the outside world, that the dream didn't let reality get the better of it.

The house phone rang as I turned the canvas back around. Now for my next trick. I grabbed a book from my bedside pile, and without thinking about it, I tore out a page and held it in my hands. I got down on my knees, because this was a sort of ritual, and it was the only position that could keep me still enough to focus. I stared at the page, concentrating, letting my heart build up to a shiver, just like it had under Li's hand. I pictured the pressure of it, tried to draw strength from that. I thought of his eyes and took a quick intake of breath — eyes that were always plunging beneath my skin and making my pulse jump. *Pulse. Pulse. Pulse . . .* I held that feeling close, tried to pump it through my fingers and into the paper. I made enough birds in the library to know the drill, but there I was being helped along by other forces. Out here it would take something extra. *Pulse. Pulse . . .*

The phone stopped ringing. A corner of the page twitched. My heart crawled into my throat—

"Ashleigh?"

Mum jolted me out of my spell casting, appearing in the open doorway. My eyes gave away scandal before I could stop them.

"What're you doing?"

"Sitting," I half-lied.

Her mouth smiled but her eyes were too tired to, detecting my mistruth. "Tabitha's on the phone for you."

She left my door frame, the thought of my refusing the

call never crossing her mind. I called after her. "Tell her I'm not here."

Mum double-took, sticking her head back into my room. "What? Why, honey?"

Hands clenching my knees again, my impatience reeled back like a wave after a firm flash of it. "I'm just kind of tired, that's all. Tell her I'll call her tomorrow."

And again, the question. The question that tested both my sanity and my state. "Are you all right, Ashleigh?"

They always assume something's wrong when it's just starting to go right.

I shook my head. "Don't worry about me. I'll call her tomorrow." Then, over my shoulder, I cast the most sincere of smiles that my mother could do nothing but trust in. She returned it, and shut my door behind her.

I got to my feet, catching the disapproval of my eyes in the vanity mirror.

"Don't look at me like that," I whispered.

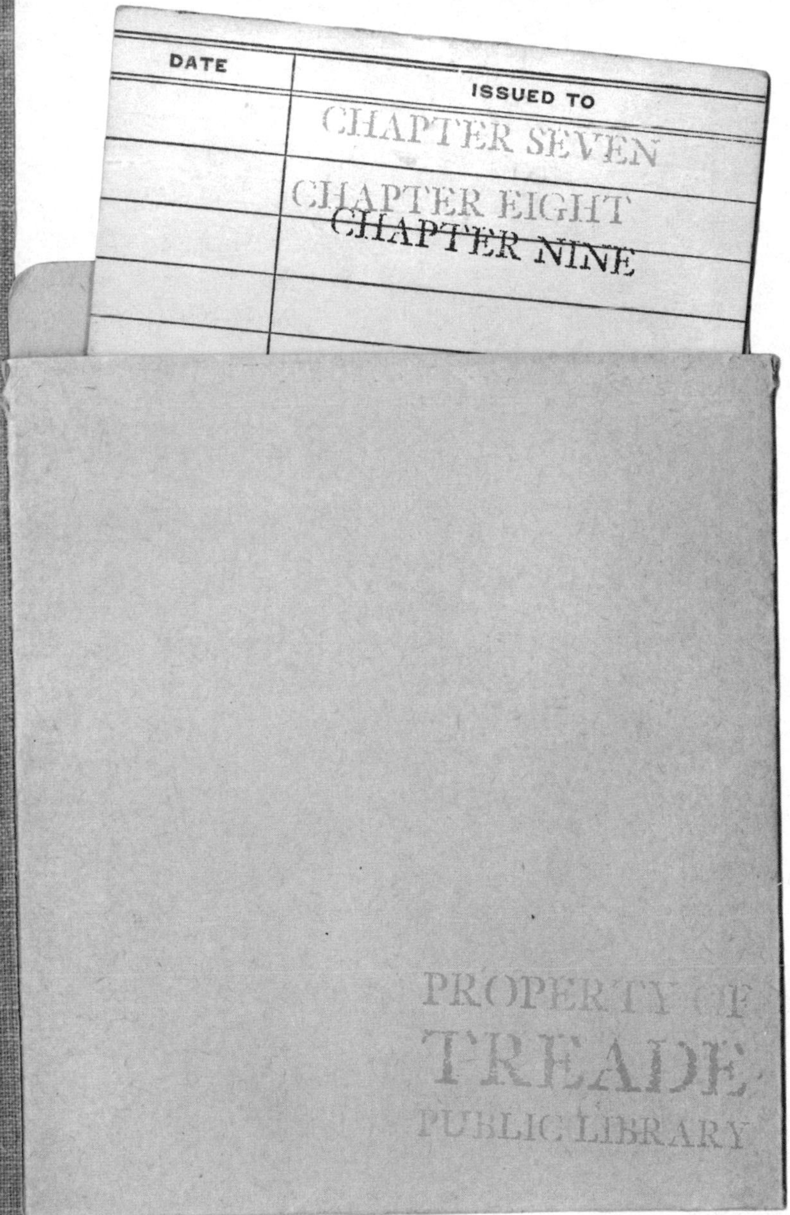
DATE
ISSUED TO
CHAPTER SEVEN
CHAPTER EIGHT
CHAPTER NINE
PROPERTY OF
TREADE
PUBLIC LIBRARY

It had only just begun, that much was true. I wanted to recapture that moment when we suddenly appeared on an ancient road in Greece, when the air itself tasted sweet and alive just by reading the words. The stories could clothe us and our moments, and we were in a mine of never-ending supply. With our hands serving as pickaxes and audacity powering us on, we went to work.

Li was in the middle of teaching the paper macaw — the one he'd spent the afternoon crafting — how to dance, while I delved into the important matter of finding us the worthiest books I could. I darted up and down the rolling ladders like a dutiful lemur, dumping piles at his feet while the rustling of parchment birds skipped behind me, clouds of them taking to the air as my piles grew and tipped over. I was treating this as very serious business, and Li could see that. He eventually left the parrot to its own devices so he could scamper after me, and he quickly turned book-finding into a competition. His pile grew to challenge mine, and we prepared to duel like the stakes were high and noon was higher.

I dove for my first selection, flipping through manically and smirking. He took on a gunslinger stance, waiting for me to start reading. *"And the crewman knew the song well, and they sang: 'Fifteen men on a dead-man's chest . . .'"*

The floor rumbled, but we were used to this now, the hardwood boards unfurling and peeling back to make room for waves and a ship's deck. The prow burst through, figurehead first, and rose out of the water like it was midresurrection. We busted hard to starboard, and Li was suddenly my crutched Long John Silver, peg leg and all. He grabbed hold of the rigging and followed me to the railing as we gazed out over the sea.

I shook my head, trying to keep my sailor's cap down tight as the salty wind made a reach for it. Absolutely every detail was vivid, everything around us taking on a sepia tone, like the pages themselves, but that just added to the atmosphere even more. "This is too much."

The deck lurched and I lost the book to the open air and the parchment seagulls floating around us. The covers snapped shut as the book hit the water, and we both tumbled to the library floor when it came back into existence to meet us.

Li reached out and dusted me off, plucking a bit of seaweed from my hair that disappeared with a gentle *pop* when he shook it off.

"It's like we're really there, every time," I trilled, slumping onto my back and staring at the peaks of the higher-than-high ceiling. I had challenged Li to see if it would be possible to make a paper sky for the paper birds, to make them feel more at home, more alive. Wrinkled parchment cirrus floated above our heads now, and had the sense to develop their own shapes and forms independent of our whims. The birds danced between them, joyous. Li watched me, instead.

"It's just too easy," I started, but he tapped my head, trying to encourage me out of my logic. "I know, I know," I said. "I can't ask how, because it isn't that simple." I shut my eyes. "Maybe it's all in our hearts, then." I turned my face to him. "But at least we can go to all these places together, right? Then I know I'm not crazy."

He smiled, giving nothing away as he pointed to my pile. I picked up the one he wanted and clambered to my feet. "Oh, good choice!"

I thumbed through and picked a page at random of *Journey to the Center of the Earth*, eyes twinkling in wonderment as the bookshelves fissured into the most beautiful rock features, the ground sloping into a subterranean ocean and the walls looming in complement as they morphed into mushrooms the size of houses. It was dark, but bioluminescent stones flickered in the cracks, highlighting Li's long-limbed grace as he bent down to touch the water. The ripple seemed to go for miles, but he pulled me close when the cry of a mastodon echoed from the black coastline miles beyond us.

"Don't worry, Axel, I'll protect you," I chided, shutting the book just as lightning cracked across the depths in front of us. As the flash subsided, we were back.

We had been going about this for the entire day, but I couldn't get enough. I jumped up and down. "It's incredible! We have to do *Tales from 1,001 Nights* next!" I shuffled through my pile, flipping through *A Child's Garden of Verses*, *The Hound of the Baskervilles*, Tennyson, Coleridge, *Alice's Adventures in Wonderland* . . . "I swear I had it here just a second ago . . ."

I looked to Li for help, but his interests had shifted. He was marvelling at my iPod, turning it over, absorbing its angles, testing the tracker wheel, and shaking it at his ear. It was an old model, all thick and with a duct-taped backing from banging it around too much. I blinked.

"I know it's old, but it still works." I went back to searching, double-taking as Li brought my ear buds an inch from his eyes.

I thought he was kidding — he *had* to be. But his face was genuinely mystified. "It's an iPod, Li." I took the ear buds away from him, leaning in and putting them carefully into his ears. I pressed play, and I thought he was going to launch out of his skin. He ripped them out of his ears and threw them at me, looking like a cat that had just been punched off a fence.

"Sorry! The volume must be up all the way . . ." I turned it off, put it away. "You really don't know what an iPod is? How long have you been cut off from the world?"

He looked particularly insulted at that, forehead creasing to a frown as he returned to digging through my bag. "Hey, c'mon, leave that stuff alone and help me." I went back to the book pile, sorting through a few, but before I could choose between *Don Quixote* and Tennyson, Li had let out a little gasp, and was pulling my sketchbook free.

I dropped both books and sprang after him, reaching. "Don't!" He pirouetted backwards onto a table, bounding far enough to keep me at bay while he browsed. What was, at first, another means of teasing me, quickly became something else. He came back my way and settled on the edge of the table, letting me boost up beside him while he flipped through the pages, touching the lines in wonderment.

Wow, he mouthed, using every minute muscle in his jaw. It felt like high praise, seeing the ghost of his awe hang there at his mouth.

"I'm not Van Gogh or anything," I shrugged, dangling my feet. He playfully pushed my shoulder and smacked the pages with the back of his hand, incredulous that I was being so humble.. I just shrugged again, nervous, smiling.

He flipped to a blank page and carefully slid the sketchbook into my lap while he sprang up, jogging backwards and, in a flourish, posing.

I giggled but put the sketchbook aside. "Maybe some other time." I was more keen to get back into the books, diving into them and feeling the worlds build up around us as I read. I swung down, but Li grabbed me by the shoulders and forced me backwards into the table. He levelled me with his eyes, very seriously, tapping my sketchbook.

"C'mon," I tried to reason. "Wouldn't you rather spend the afternoon in Arabia? Or Avalon?" I looked away, but he guided us eye to eye with his hand at my chin. He wouldn't let it go. I blushed.

Holding his hands up in a *stop* motion, he bounded to my bag, stuck his hand in, and produced a pencil. Taking the sketchbook in his arms, he started scribbling, and my heart jittered as he forced it back on me.

The letters were crooked, the words messy, but it felt like I was hearing his voice for the first time, loud and clear. "*This is your kind of magic,*" it said.

Putting the pencil in my hand, he got on his knees and whimpered like a puppy. If his words didn't break me, his face did. I couldn't keep my smile down. "Okay, okay." I finally gave in, throwing my hands up in the air. "But you'll probably want to sit."

His teeth flashed in a grin and he bounded up, showboating with a chair until he settled on it, making a fine impression of an aristocrat as he adjusted his collar, unrolled his sleeves, and buttoned the cuffs. He smoothed his chest down and placed a hand over his heart — poised like a gentleman sitting for his portrait photograph. A curt nod to say *I'm ready now*, and I rolled my eyes, mocking, and dove in.

Lines and curves started appearing under my hand. A book-page moth landed on the corner of the paper and I brushed it away, only half-aware of it. I decided that I'd only try to tackle his face, but even still capturing Li at all was like grabbing for dandelion fluff just out of my reach. "This is the first time I've ever seen you sit still," I murmured, my eyes snapshotting every single one of his details. Short of a laugh, he barely stirred.

It was raw, at first. The outline of the face was mild, relaxed, long but not too broad. The mane of the young adventurer curved up at the nape of his neck, fanning gently like damp feathers, starlit sheen dancing in the curls. I stippled around the curves of his cheeks and mouth, that slight bit of stubble needing definition. His eyes stayed on me, intense as always. My heart sped up, but I tried to focus on the task at hand. His posture was relaxed and muted as I drew the rest of him beyond his shoulders. He was entranced — not by the vanity of being reproduced — but by me. I beat myself up for thinking of *Titanic* and all it implied right at that moment. At least he was clothed, and we weren't about to drown in the Atlantic.

Each time I looked up from the page, the rest of him was wholly still, but not the eyes. They flickered over me, seemingly searching my now flailing heart as it climbed into my throat, and by this time, he had to know he was the reason.

I was pleased enough with having captured all his many details, until our copper sun flickered against something at Li's throat. I blinked and realized that it was a golden medallion, and I added it quickly to the drawing.

My pencil stopped when I was satisfied, and when the attention got to be too much. But as I exhaled and leaned back, there he was. Eyes and grin shaped by graphite under my hands, and the likeness was good, but it did zero honest justice to my Li. *My* Li. I felt more nervous about exhibiting this to my audience of one than I had about bringing a world to life with words just a few minutes ago.

My subject had slipped out of his chair right in front of me, and as usual, I didn't hear him creep up at all. I pressed the sketchbook to my chest. "Now don't expect anything amazing, I've got a lot to learn, still."

But his expression, more sober than usual, was a wordless reassurance from his shining grey irises, hushing my worry as he lowered the sketchbook. He was plainly taken aback, bending closer to the paper as if it was a mirror. As if he had truly been *seen* for the first time.

I leaned forwards, looking with him. "Is it . . . okay?"

Cheekbones drawing up, his smile forced me to clear my throat and look up all the way. "I'll clean it up a little later, when I'm home." In the clouds we had made, there was a small golden sun that I didn't remember making. I watched it glint as it shifted. "I was thinking of going to the University of Manitoba to study art," I found myself saying, and was surprised by it, because I'd never articulated these dreams to anyone else. "But most of all, I would give anything to build a story like the ones we jump into. To shape these worlds and live in them forever." I shut my eyes. "Then I could stay *here* forever. In a way."

Li was gazing thoughtfully at the sketch, but his head lifted slowly as I spoke. I waved away the gravity of his stare. "Anyway. What about you? What do you want to be when you . . . well, not when you grow up. But you know what I mean."

Bending down over our pile of books, he grabbed for and flipped through *Le Morte d'Arthur*, marking a page with his finger as he passed it to me.

"Lancelot?" I said, looking down at the indelible ink word and back up to Li. He struck a pose, and for a second the light of our false sun struck him, and around the edges he seemed to be wearing a gleaming breastplate and hoisting a long sword in the air. I snorted and the metal faded.

"Lancelot is a paragon, but he was *flawed*. You remind me more of this guy." I shuffled through a dainty copy of Coleridge's works, landing on an illustration that looked like it had been rendered in stained glass. It accompanied one of my favourite poems: "Love," the tale of the minstrel who sang stories to a girl, and hid his love inside them.

Oft in my waking dreams do I
Live o'er again that happy hour,
When midway on the mount I lay,
Beside the ruin'd tower.

There was a tower, all right, and it flickered into view behind us. Half of it had been eroded away by time, or else, the idea of time, and we huddled against it in the waist-high grass. In front of us was the statue of the knight, in my arms was a lute, Li holding the book open for me as I strummed — and my fingers had minds of their own, building a melody from the heart of me. But this was a story within a story, the stone knight bursting to life and performing the sad deeds of the song for us. He lay dying in the lap of his lady, and he muttered something we couldn't hear. Li put his arm around me and his head on my shoulder as the song ended. And we sat like this awhile, leaning on one another, listening to the wind.

By the time I got home, I had four missed calls and two voice-mails. I had forgotten my cell was even with me. I deleted them immediately, unprepared for the guilt they'd surely leave me with. I had missed dinner — but then again, I usually did, since Mum was on a string of night shifts and I was too busy revelling in the freedom of her absence to care. I had left the iPod behind for Li to play with, but the drawing stayed in my keeping. I tucked it into the corner of my mirror, smoothing it out and getting lost in his eyes. I'd work on it later.

I went to my canvas treasure trove and hid more reclaimed Polaroids behind it. They were my windows into dream memories, the ones I could capture, at least, and even though they were right in front of me, I wondered if they'd happened at all. The photos helped me breathe a little easier, even though both Li and I were dealing in borrowed time. I knew that I wouldn't be able to escape for long, that there was soon to be a crater where the library now stood, and that one day we would both be locked out of our den of dreams.

And what would happen to Li once I left? My chest lurched. No matter what happened to the library, I actually had a time bomb strapped to me, a definite end point I couldn't control. I knew I would have to tell him soon; his haunted eyes when I had been *late* were bad enough, but the way the library itself had reacted was even worse. What would happen if I had never come back? I felt like Treade had spun a web and caught me in it just as I was set on my getaway. I thought that the only way I could survive and build a true dream was to get out. But it was here all along, and I couldn't leave it behind.

I stumbled to conceal my photographic menagerie as suddenly, rudely, a knock came on my open door. Paul.

"Surprise!" He straightened out of his exaggerated pose.

I was quickly getting tired of these surprises. "How did you get in here?" I accused immediately, leaving no room to even pretend I was happy to see him.

He stiffened, raising an eyebrow. "Your mom let me in."

It was my turn to frown. "No, she didn't. The house is empty."

"Ash," he said, pronouncing every syllable as if I couldn't understand him. "She's just downstairs."

I darted my head into the hall. Sure enough, a plume of smoke was dangling over her head, and she smiled at me from her chair. "Sweetie, I've been calling you and calling you. Didn't you hear me?"

I felt a wave of cold ebb over me. She hadn't been there. The house had been so quiet that my ears were ringing. But she was there. And so was Paul. I had forgotten, for that second, that he was there, too. I was forgetting a lot of things.

"Oh. Well . . ." I went back into my room, feeling like I was emerging from a catatonic state.

Paul floated in behind me. "I know it goes without saying, but you've been acting weirder than usual, Ash."

In the intervening seconds as an excuse became lodged in my throat, Paul touched the drawings and book excerpts I had pasted to the wall, pausing to read one of the poems I'd rewritten there in Sharpie. There was a time when I thought maybe Paul and I could date — it seemed like the next logical step after so long, even though we dreamed in separate directions. But he wasn't my sterling knight, my curly haired, silent bard, my bird-making magician man, and no one would be able to live up to that, least of all Paul. My chest tightened, the shattered shards of my sentimental thoughts of Paul worrying into the corners of my patience.

"I tried calling but your phone was off again," he explained, not bothering to justify the accusation in his voice as he turned to face me. "We haven't seen you in a while, and you've been acting really off. We were wondering what was up."

I realized my fists were coiled at my side like pressurized hearts. It took a conscious effort to release them, lifting them heavily to rest on my canvas, protectively. *We* were wondering. *We* noticed. They were ganging up on me, slowly, quietly.

"Nothing's up," I said. The words were heavy and clipped.

Paul shuffled his feet. Luckily for me, he wasn't the type to talk about feelings. He folded his arms. "Are you sure? Tabitha and I—"

"—are worried. I know. I get it." The brush-off jumped out of me, propelled by that dark, insidious thing that had taken root beneath my bones. "I'm fine. I'm just busy. You guys don't have to check up on me."

My eyes felt heavy all of a sudden, and I could see Paul's mouth working around his last attempt at concern, but all I could hear was a rushing sound, like water spilling down a wall . . .

"Ash?"

I snapped to. Paul had moved to my mirror and was sliding the drawing out of its place for a closer look.

"This new?"

I grabbed for it, but he held fast to an end. It was mine and no one else's, all of it, and I wouldn't let him wreck it. I snatched hard, and a good half of it ripped away.

"Paul!"

The paper ripping stabbed at me like grindstone-fresh pins. I clenched the pieces close to my chest, and tears of hatred struck. The water in my eyes turned the world into an aquarium, and past the tears I could see he was sorry, but I blocked it out.

"How could you do that? What's wrong with you?"

"I'm . . . I'm sorry, Ash. You can fix it, can't you?"

"You don't get it, do you?" I unveiled a hissing sneer that I had no idea I was capable of. *"It won't be the same."*

I stormed to my night table drawer, slamming the remains of my beautiful Li into the dark.

Paul tried to cool the sharp air suspended between us. "Who was that? In the . . . drawing, I mean."

"I'm tired," I snapped. "I'll call you tomorrow, okay?"

"But . . . Ash, I'm—"

I prickled deeper. "Just go," the thing inside of me seethed.

He backed into the doorway, but he didn't trust my conviction. I turned and gave him a Medusa glare, tears instantly dried. I cracked a smile, but it wasn't mine.

"I promise," I heard myself saying. "I'm fine. The move is just stressing me out more than I thought it would. Don't worry about me, okay? I'll see you guys soon."

That pacified him. Even though his smile was weak, he accepted it.

"Well, okay," he shuffled his feet again. "I'll text you. And . . . I'm sorry about the picture."

"Don't worry about me," I repeated.

I could hear him pick his way down the stairs, happy to leave me to brood in the lake of lies pooling quickly at my feet. I could hear Mum having a brief word with him, her racking cough echoing over the conversation as she asked

Paul how his mom was. At least I thought that's what they were saying; the water sound was rising again, and I tuned them out as I slid my night table drawer open. The paper-thin moment that Li and I had built sat rumpled and ruined, right down the middle.

It's only paper, the ghost of my reason whispered.

But I'd drawn blood with it, anyway.

Everything is going along too smoothly and she is convinced it will go wrong very soon, but she pushes that miserable thought as far back as it can go.

"Wow, they sure got it up in a hurry, didn't they?" her son breathes in wonder, helping her out of the car to marvel at their work. She leans carefully against his shoulder and, shielding her eyes, joins him in gazing.

"The most enthusiastic contractors come out of Treade, darling, since they seldom get to work on anything quite like this."

The building itself hadn't been the issue from inception onwards; it was securing the small tract of Hoban Wilson's land on the outskirts of his coveted woods that had been the true test. Wilson claimed that there was something about this forest, something ancient and precious presiding here that would only take being tainted so far. "My family has been custodians of these trees for going on seventy years now, before this town was a town." He had stomped his cane for emphasis at that. "These woods keep their own counsel, and they'd be damned to keep yours, too." He went on to swear up and down that if her intentions hadn't been at least *partway* noble, he would never have given her the half acre he so graciously let go of. She was fairly certain it was less her intentions and more her money that had whittled him down, in the end. Forest custodian or no, Hoban Wilson was still human. She remained confident that before the decade was out, he'd be selling these trees hand over fist, what with a war brewing overseas and the economy turning.

They cross the grounds, her on his arm, him leading her like the gentleman he is close to becoming. She beams up at him, pulling at the fringe of his curls. "It's so soft; it feels like your baby hair."

He purses his lips, grinning. "Now, now, Mother. I'll cut it when I take the big business mantle. Until then, I get to keep the curls. The girls like 'em." He winks and she nudges him playfully.

The tang of sawdust and the bitter scent of pine enrobe them as they confer with the project manager. The building will be done by week's end, the door having arrived from Vancouver just last night, covered, as it is, in the intricate tapestry of mythological bodies swimming upstream against their own stories. It was commissioned by an artist on the West Coast, the entire composition of the door reclaimed driftwood, moulded and shaped by the sea.

"The wall shelves are being installed as we speak, but the standing cases won't be ready for another week — we've had some trouble with the supplier in Winnipeg. Care to take a look inside and see how it's coming?"

She raises her hands, feinting back a step before the threshold. "Old family superstition," she explains. "Can't go in until the door has been properly put on. Something about crossing over into the veil of another world. My Baba and her Ukrainian paranoia ran deep."

Her son claps the contractor encouragingly on the shoulder. "We trust it will be splendid. And we can't wait to share it with the rest of the town."

After the last brief bit of news — looking over the individual petal panes that would make up the facing vestibule window — she relaxes under a nearby tree, taking the proffered sandwich from the basket he had brought with them. Reclining, they watch the sun climb.

"I didn't think it would come together so seamlessly," he admits with partial sheepishness. "The entire thing is like a dream."

She sighs, absorbing the splendour of the very air. "One thing I can give credence to about the sordid things that brought us here," and she shifts her tired face to his, "is that we could make something of it."

He chews thoughtfully on a cracker. "Now *this* is the kind of legacy a man can be proud of. The kind Father ought to have had. The factories, all the backdoor deals. He was in the business of feeding a country; it was a noble work, but he lost sight of what he was doing. It devoured him."

"And while your father fed grain to western Canada, you will feed them stories?" she asks, and he taps his nose.

"Stories were the original manna," and now he's waxing poetical, which he knows gets a rise out of her.

"My son, the dizzy dreamer. Girls want to marry doctors and businessmen, not tellers of tales."

He shakes a finger at her, chiding. "Now we both know Father hooked you with a poem. The dreaming is sadly hereditary."

It is a good day, so far. She can feel her breath rattling less, feel the ripples in her ventricles as a hum and less a clatter. Maybe she can live through this after all; here, in the last of the summer sun, watching their endeavour rise up from nothing, she is convinced that anything can be possible. For a price.

She pulls up a clump of grass, testing the waters. "About your birthday, darling . . ."

He sighs through his nose. "We really don't have to go to the trouble you're planning for it. A soiree, all those narrow-minded socialites from the city—"

"Watch yourself," she warns, "you're speaking to a girl who made her living at being a socialite."

He scowls. "You and I both know that you don't compare to those preening busybodies. And I don't know that it's doing your health any good to be getting this worked up about martinis and swanning around in a place that has no use for either." His slender fingers push back his sunlight-kissed hair. "I don't want Jovan Grain, Mother. Running this business has never been for me, even my father knew that. There are other men who can have it grow in their hands."

"Lesser men," she scoffs, but at first she doesn't retaliate. It is not in his temperament to be shut up in an office, in the same way she never did well being a kept woman. He longs to walk along the lake on the other side of town, to write his musings in the sand and let them wash away. He has wanderlust in his soul, just like she once did, before the entire affair got away from her. Before her body abandoned her and her soulmate drowned himself in his work.

"Perhaps you're right. We should give it over to someone else, someday," and she stretches back, shutting her eyes. "In the meantime, we need a means to keep our dreams alive, my dear. Sometimes we must sacrifice a bit of ourselves to earn those moments that make us incandescent."

Quiet now, pulling her silk, tasselled shawl back up to her shoulders, he simply murmurs, "Who's the teller of tales now, Mama?"

She laughs. They spend the rest of the daylight revelling, for at their feet, their legacy rises out of the woods.

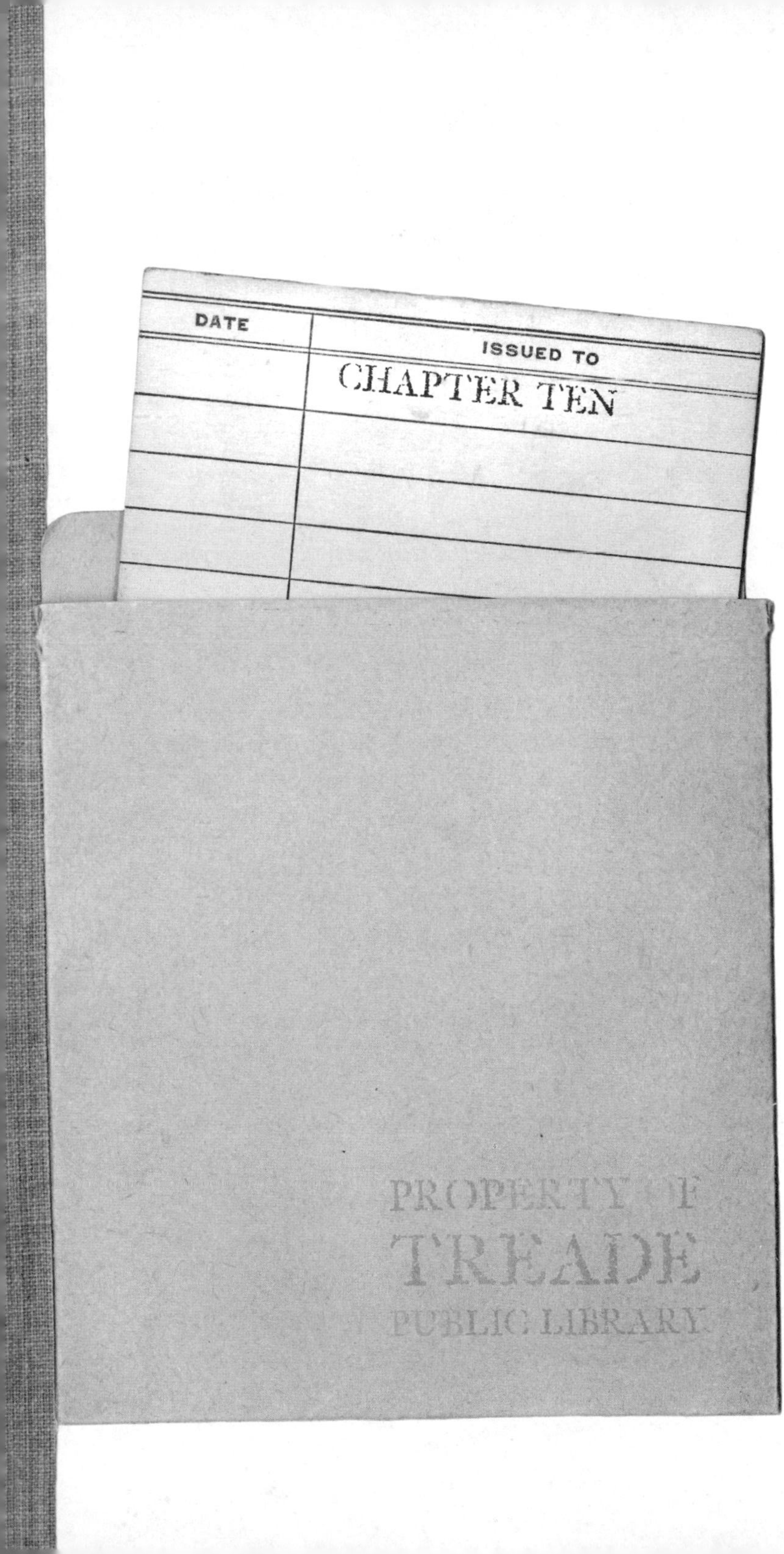
DATE
ISSUED TO
CHAPTER TEN
PROPERTY
TREADE
PUBLIC LIBRARY

I rubbed my eyes and staved off a yawn as I sat cross-legged on one of the reading tables, sketching the deer clock frantically. I had created a few of these drawings now, desperate to reclaim what I'd felt in reproducing Li yesterday, his words etched on a page and over my soul: *This is* your *kind of magic*. I sat and waited for him, this being the first time since we'd met that I had truly shown up first.

I hadn't slept at all last night, the only lights shining against the velvet sky the floodlights on the grain elevator. I stared for hours at the shadows they cast onto my floor, lying in bed and listening, at first, to my mother coughing down the hall, and then plagued by the water sound in the back of my ears. I figured that this was a normal phenomena, just like when you hear a consistent ringing for no real reason, but it was oddly comforting, the tone of it like a small swell lapping against a rock, over and over. I followed its cadence and let it take my troubled thoughts: how I felt for pushing Paul away, how I had plainly ignored my mother's presence . . . how every day at home and out of the library made me feel like I was sleepwalking. As the night deepened, my subconscious became infected by the vision of books floating in Lake Jovan, bobbing to the surface and stuck in the reeds. I reached for them, but they sank away. And there was that woman, white haired and floating among them, but she was reaching for me, instead.

There were a few paper birds hanging about the stacks, but not the flocks that usually did. And those that I saw were sleeping, little folded heads tucked under wafer-thin feathers. It seemed that, without both of us, the library functioned at a halfway point potential.

Something heavy fell on the other side of the room. I lurched up.

"Li?"

I uncurled my legs from under me and slid off the table. I trod lightly, knowing that this had to be another one of his games, his tricks, but I was poised for flight anyway. I searched row by row until I came upon the source of the noise; there were a handful of books on the floor, looking as if they'd been pulled from the shelves. I started putting them back into the holes they'd made, but as I did so, I realized that the shelf right next to them was a *trompe l'oeil*, just like the vault of the library's ceiling — books painted deftly on the flat wall, a perfect imitation. I ran my hand down the place where the optical illusion met the real shelves and found a seam. A door. It was slightly ajar, and when I looked down there was a puddle of water gathering at the threshold.

I swallowed, once more calling Li's name, wanting to be sure he was on the other side. I'd been seeing, and hearing, so much water lately, that I was beginning to think it signified something sinister, something I didn't yet understand.

"If you're trying to scare me," I said in an attempt to convince myself, "it's your most feeble attempt yet."

I pushed the door open a crack just so I could see inside. It was completely dark. I peered in, and seeing that there wasn't any kind of light inside, I opened the door wider to let the small amount of library light shine in. It was a small room, kind of like the hidden sitting room upstairs, but there was nowhere to sit, and it wasn't nearly as inviting. The carpet was rotting, the wallpaper bubbling and peeling, and there was a consistent series of drips coming from the ceiling. This had to be the worst-kept room in the library, considering how every other part of it glowed like a rococo dreamscape.

But the waterlogged crown moulding wasn't what got my attention; there was some kind of portrait hanging on the back wall. It was medium-sized and pictured a woman; she was swan slight and long limbed, with wheat-coloured hair. She had an amusement to her grey eyes as she sat by a window, a book turned face down in her lap and her mouth parted in a laugh. She was beautiful. I stepped in, entranced. My footsteps squished on the wet carpet as I moved in for a closer look. The painting was in nearly perfect condition, compared to everything else in the room, but when I got up to it, I realized that the woman wasn't alone. She was holding the hand of someone, a small child, maybe, but that part of the canvas had been bubbled up and eaten away. It was hard to tell anything else, and when I reached up to touch the brush strokes, a huge dollop of water hit the back of my outstretched hand. I jumped back and tried to look past the gloom to see any hint of the source, but what really made me leap out of my skin was that the sliver of light coming in from the hall behind me was shrinking. Someone was closing the door.

"Hey!" I said, springing towards it, the water now running in tear-streaked rivulets down the walls, the wallpaper swelling under it. I grabbed the door by its edge, pulling hard and fighting against the person on the other side.

"This isn't funny, Li, it's dark in here!"

Something bumped against my ankle. I looked down and saw that, in the rising water at my feet, a book bobbed to the surface, and one I had seen already. A silver cover, winking at me, followed by other books clotting the floor. I didn't have enough hands to reach out and grab the silver book, and just as the struggle turned in my favour, I looked out through the crack between the door and the jamb, thinking that if I showed Li the anxiety stamped into my face, he would give me some pity.

But it was not Li's face I saw on the other side of the door in that split second before I won; it was the face I'd tried to part yards of white hair from, the face at the bottom of the lake. Her flesh was fish white, her eyes whiter still, and what was worse was that I recognized her from somewhere else as our gazes locked. I kept pulling, and in a single blink she was gone from the other side of the door, and now inside the room with me. I hadn't even have a chance to shriek before the door swung out, and I pitched forwards, flat on my face in the bookcase aisle. The *trompe l'oeil* door slammed shut behind me.

I bolted, tripping to my feet. *"Li!"*

I raced out of the row and ploughed directly into him; he had been running towards my voice, but he caught me like a skilled quarterback before I could knock both of us over.

"You're here," I panted, half-collapsing in his arms. I jerked out of them the instant that the woman's face flashed back into my mind. "There's someone else here, Li! Did you see her come this way?"

He shushed me, a hand stroking my hair as he shook his head. I grabbed his hand and dragged him back the way I'd come. "Come here and look. It was right here . . . *she* was right here. You have to see this room."

But when we got there, the door was gone, in its place an actual shelf filled with actual books. And the floor was conspicuously dry.

Li touched the bookcase and looked at me, shrugging. I felt worse than insane. I felt like the library had just turned on me. "But it was here!" I cried, starting to tear books right from the wall as I felt for a seam. "Right here . . ."

He turned me away, shushing me again as he got to his knees in front of me. *Relax*, his face asserted, taking a deep breath and making me mimic him. Leading me back to where there was light and twenty paper cockatiels tumbling and flirting in the paper sky, he boosted me onto the table beside my sketchbook, feeling my forehead for fever.

"I'm not sick." I slapped his hand away, feeling sheepish and embarrassed. "I really saw someone. She was . . ." I couldn't even say the word. My heart was still hammering in my ears. *She was dead.*

He pursed his lips like a sad puppy, then reached around me for my sketchbook, scribbling something on a fresh page. *I have a surprise for you.* He waggled his eyebrows for effect.

I blinked, "A surprise? Like I need another one . . ."

Wagging a *no no* finger at me, he motioned for me to stand up, and rolling my eyes, I obeyed. He then covered his eyes and gestured at me to copy.

I was hesitant, at first, on that last one. "What if that freaky woman pops up again? Will you protect me?"

Li scratched his temple until his eyes lit in epiphany. He starting unbuttoning his collar, and as I stiffened in apprehension of what exactly he was doing, he pulled out the medallion I had seen earlier when I was drawing him. He slipped it over his head and let it dangle between us. It glinted and spun, hypnotising, then he undid the clasp, and without warning, leaned in to fasten it around my neck.

"Oh, Li, I couldn't—"

He shushed me with a whisper as he fiddled with the clasp, and after a momentary lapse in his usually nimble fingers, he drew away.

I fingered the medallion. Emblazoned on the front of it was St. Anthony. I turned it over, but it was scuffed and worn. I ran my finger over one scuff that looked like it could have once been a cursive *L*, but I wasn't sure.

"St. Anthony. Patron saint of lost things." I laughed, looking shyly up at him. "Li, it's . . . it's beautiful. But I can't take this."

He put a finger to his lips as if to shush me again, then leaned down and kissed the medal. His hands laid solidly on my shoulders, and I understood the gesture. *For protection.*

I couldn't control my skin from prickling and turning red from the heat of his stare. I fiddled with the chain. "Thank you." I smiled, trying to reclaim the humour. "It's a nice surprise, really."

At that he wagged his finger and mouthed *ah ah!* This wasn't the surprise. He bade me, again, to shut my eyes. "Okay, okay . . ." I sighed and did as I was told.

I heard his running footsteps scuffle away, unable to picture what he could have planned, because the possibilities were endless. I couldn't help but smile, wrapping my fingers around his medallion and feeling calmer already. A gift *and* a surprise. He had done something just for me, he had been thinking of me . . . just knowing that made me feel better, momentarily forgetting the terror I'd felt moments earlier — *if it had happened at all*, I thought. I was reciting that so often day-to-day that now it had become a mantra, a double-edged comfort; if it hadn't happened, then I had nothing to worry about. But these sorts of things kept happening, which meant that some part of me was going mad, or I had fallen down the kind of rabbit hole from which I could never re-emerge.

A paper bird landed on my shoulder. I heard it before I felt it, the tiny thing being as fragile as it was. I couldn't help but open my eyes and smile at it, until another landed on the opposite shoulder. And another. And another. Soon there were at least twenty, thirty book-page birds clinging to the back of my shirt, making me bend forward to accommodate them. Though I was giggling, I couldn't help but feel perplexed. And then I saw Li below me, twirling and fanning his arms like a boisterous conductor, the birds on my back and shoulders swaying with his hands.

I flushed. "What are you doing?"

He just grinned and swooned on, flicking his wrists. And then I could see it; the birds were unfolding back into their original shapes, but then the pages inverted on themselves, transforming again. They folded, they lengthened, and they nestled between my shoulder blades as they layered one on top of the other. The weight sat concentrated there until, Li spreading his hands wide, they unfurled.

Paper wings. And they were mine.

I put a hand to my mouth, neck craning hard to believe

what I was seeing. One wing gave an experimental flick, and I felt the warmth of them dazzle up my spine. Yes, I could *feel* them, I could move them. Which meant—

"Can I fly?"

Li bowed, his eyes still locked on mine, twinkling. A current of paper birds swirled over him as they asserted his own pair of wings. He bowed, as if to say, *like so,* and he sprang into the air, somersaulting and landing ever so lightly at my side, lifting me to my feet, then taking both my hands in his and holding them to his chest. This was all for my sake; the total world immersion, our handmade sky, this constant dream that we were sharing. It was a daily gift of gratitude for something I had no idea I did. And Li wasn't about to tell me what that was, either.

I flushed deeper, feeling his eyes above me and the light from the sun we made casting momentary rainbows on us. "You'll be close by, right?"

Letting go of one hand, he semicrouched, eyes never leaving mine. *Always.*

I crouched down, too, my wings shivering in anticipation. We looked up into our sky, clouds parting to reveal infinite blue. This newly fashioned world was ours, all ours.

We took to the sky, library melting away behind us into nothing but dawn. We were inhabiting our own story, now.

· ○ ● ○ ●

I seemed to stop dreaming at night. No dreams of a drowned woman, of books dotting the surface of Lake Jovan, no one reaching out to shut the door and lock me inside someone else's memory. This suited me fine; I felt like I was dreaming so much during the days that I was drunk on them, and come nightfall I needed the break. I'd rather live in dreams than see them leave with the sunrise, anyway.

I found my finger retracing steps again, passing in a circle over the rim of my mug, eyes and thoughts lost in the bronze ocean of my tea. I was engulfed in the memory of yesterday, of doing the impossible, of flying. But it would have been nothing without Li's hand in mine as we soared so high that we danced with the stars. Just like my princess painting.

"Paul stopped by again," Mum said after clearing her rattling throat, seating herself across from me and jolting me instantly back to reality. As I watched her fill a vase and place it, daisies and all, in front of me, I tried hard to convince myself that she had been there, in the kitchen, all along.

I took a deep gulp of tea. "Mm-hm?"

"Did you three get into some kind of fight?" She slid the notion slyly into the conversation. I could feel my face darkening, but I laughed as though it was unheard of.

"Well!" she sighed. "I was only asking. You seem like you're avoiding them."

"I'm just . . . busy." I feebly shrugged.

"Well, if you haven't seen Paul or Tabitha lately, where is it you've been going these days? I barely see you, and what little I do, you're off in la-la land."

"Everyone's so sad already," I heard the words ooze out, not conscious that I had formed them in my head, "and it's only going to get sadder. I think it'll make it easier on us if we don't spend every waking moment together before it all has to end."

She tilted her head. "But they're your best friends, love."

I have a friend. More than that. And he is all I will ever need. The thought hissed through to my core, and for a second I thought I had said actually said it, it was so loud.

"We all have to grow up sometime." I waved her off, getting up to put my mug in the sink. The faucet was dripping, the cadence matching the water I'd been ankle deep in only yesterday. I saw the room, and the portrait, as plain as if they were in front of me, and I couldn't help but give myself up a little.

"You know that building outside the park, right?"

Her index and thumb to her temple, stretching her eye upwards, she nodded. "You three have only been going there since you could run."

I swallowed, treading thinly. "The people who owned it, who built it. What happened to them?"

Taking the rest of her tea in a mouthful, she frowned. "I remember . . . someone told me it was some kind of accident. But the family didn't stay here for long. Anyway. Can't really say for sure, sweetie. All I know is that the town inherited the rights to it and the land, and that it's been condemned for years. I'm just glad they're finally getting rid of it."

Over the years, I'd always resisted finding out the answers to the building, our "place," even despite the obvious fire-wrecked roadblocks. It was Treade's diminished riddle, and I always shied away from unravelling it, even if I could. There had been magic in the place even before I knew it was a library, before I knew what kind of enchantment it held. I didn't want that spell to be broken, and now, more than ever, that was key. I did not want to be grounded in the reality I was desperately trying to escape.

So I shrugged, leaving the kitchen, Mum's reminder of "You know, you should really start packing, Ashleigh" lost on deaf ears, the sound of rushing water coming to my rescue as I clutched the golden medallion around my neck.

DATE
ISSUED TO
CHAPTER TEN
CHAPTER ELEVEN
PROPERTY OF
TREADE
PUBLIC LIBRARY

The days began melting together, blurring the lines between one and the next. The act of getting out of bed, getting dressed, declaring my leaving, and racing off, was purely instinctual, and the world outside the library disappeared from my mind the moment I entered my — *our* — palace. Games and stories enfolded us, and soon the books only served as inspiration as, with our own hands, we built a place entirely separate from them. We soared from peak to valley, dashed from ship to open sea, arm in arm as we burst through the fabric of nothing into ecstasy. We built personalities to suit each occasion, leaping from thieves to kings, pirates to jesters. When we so chose, we assumed more familiar personas, too; Li was my Hook, I his Wendy; he the Priam to my Paris, Minstrel to my Genevieve. We opened pages like we'd opened doors, prancing in to take each world hostage.

Li had given me a kind of strength that I had been missing, a conviction that what we shared was deserved, and long-awaited. Most of all, we felt secure in the presence of each other, revelling as we did in snow showers made of book pages, or chasing each other through the measureless expanse that the library had the potential to be. The truth was, for any of this to work, we needed to rely entirely on one another, to cross into each other over a bridge made of tender threads, despite how hard they quivered thinking of when we'd have to be apart. How long could a story, strung entirely from the scraps of a hundred others, really last? Could we one day just shut the page and stay tucked inside, with reality left none the wiser?

There was a special place in my head where all these thoughts collected; a dark mental cellar that had a hard padlock to it. The thoughts piled up there, and, if I put all my power into ignoring them, I could be with Li. It kept the lens of our wayfaring focused, kept me balanced and certain, and it fleshed out the corners of our story so well that I became convinced that Treade, the place where I kept leaving my friends and family, was the real dream. And that dream was the enemy.

We read, we laughed, we played. We would test each other at sword point, race on paper horseback, swoon around a dance floor at a masquerade. He would hold me down and tickle me if he couldn't get his way, and I would buck free, taking off into the air as we hopped from the chandeliers like they were lily pads. He would snatch me bodily, clean and precise, and I trusted myself in his arms to wherever we might land. We were free to lose ourselves in moments like these. We could be anything we wanted, and live on in each other.

But we weren't so active every waking second. We took our respite from epic battles, Cinderella whirlwinds, and the ziggurats of El Dorado, to the secret room upstairs, bringing books of poetry and the quieter stuff along with us. We retreated into meadows and the forests beneath the lines, listening for infinity. J.M. Barrie and T.S. Eliot took our hands and warmed us beyond the words. Poe startled with a deep antagonism that sought to manage insanity. And we tread lightly, picking our way through the land of Tír na nóg, land of eternal youth and beauty, hoping that it could preserve us and keep us. I wanted to dive into Xanadu, but Li seemed to be saving it for the right moment. I wanted badly to fall into the caverns and the pleasure-dome that Sam left behind for us, and I wondered what might have happened had he continued dreaming. How far would Kubla have gone if he hadn't been woken? If Coleridge taught me anything, it was that there was always someone waiting to spoil your best dream.

Each day I tried to stay a little longer, playing and pretending for just an hour more, but my phone would always go off — much to Li's dismay — and I would be at a loss. Each time we had to part, his face would slacken and his mind would retreat elsewhere. He would sometimes try to convince me to stay overnight, which I knew would never fly, or he would go to great lengths to hide the exit. Once, he nearly succeeded. He was getting better, every day, at making the library bend to his will.

"Li, I really have to go home," I had said, my phone ringing constantly, though every time I answered it, the signal would drop. He followed me as I made my way to the porthole, but there was a solid wall where it had been. When I whirled at Li for an answer, he just smiled benignly, taking me by the hands and trying to pull me back into the library. I wanted to stay, I would have given everything to, but I couldn't.

"Please give it back," I asked, eyes turned away from his, which, every time we went through this, grew more and more hurtful. My only comfort was that the next time we saw each other, the hurt would be forgotten, replaced by a great and terrible relief. But I could plainly see the relief hid something else; he was thinking of a way to suspend time and keep me here with him. Knowing him, and knowing what he could do, a part buried deep inside me prayed he could come up with a way to do it, before it was too late.

Treade lurked in the background of our story, weighing me down and berating me as soon as I came back into it, even though I tried everything to keep it at bay. I kept shutting my entire self off to it, and eventually, after not returning their calls, I finally managed to shake Tabitha and Paul. The odd text message here and there reminded me that they still existed, but otherwise I was shedding the contemptible weight of their love, and I floated lighter through the world because of it. My defiance rose like a swell and cleansed me of them.

But my mother wore hardest on me. She was on me for not having packed, for moving day getting closer and leaving her with all the work to do. She was agitated and short with me, when I noticed her at all, and she threatened to have me followed if I didn't start taking responsibility for my constant absences. She was worried, she was concerned. Her coughing got worse and her ashtray overflowed. I became the tic at her mouth, the tremor in her hands, but I tried to convince myself everything was fine. She was an insistent blip on my sonar, just like Tabitha and Paul, and all three of them would never understand what I was clinging to so desperately.

I never fought with my mother in all the years we shared; we were too much alike, and when we had our moments, they were petty and silly. We always understood each other and shared equal ground, no matter what. But it felt almost natural to get into snarling matches with her now, since the frequency with which we fought was amplified with each passing day. Doors slamming, words thrown like bitter hatchets. We were getting too good at it.

"You're ignoring your friends, and now you're ignoring me," she forced, frustration heavy from the other side of my closed door. Discouraged, her last assault would be a storm of coughing, but if I concentrated hard enough, I brought up the sound of water rippling around my ears, and I was safe from any guilt.

They couldn't understand. They've had me for so long, had all of my time and focus. Li had not been so fortunate. Without me he had nothing, that was plain enough. Couldn't they let me devote these last days to him? *It will all end so soon.* Last days, last moments. All of my lasts belonged to Li.

I had taken to staring dazedly at myself in the mirror. Dancing deep down in my pupils was something I recalled as reason, and she looked back at me with disappointment. The dark thing that had proliferated inside me, the thing that made me feel better about Treade's final injustices, scowled back at that disappointment and snuffed it into oblivion.

No one understood what was really going on. Not even me.

DATE
ISSUED TO
CHAPTER TEN
CHAPTER ELEVEN
CHAPTER TWELVE
PROPERTY OF
TREADE
PUBLIC LIBRARY

MMoving day was in two weeks, and today I had to tell him. Pretending that I wasn't leaving Treade for good was a lie, and I had used up most of them on my mother and my friends. I couldn't keep it up. It was tearing apart my insides to have to do it, and every cell in my body calcified against going through with the truth. Telling myself that the library would be torn down even if I stayed made it worse, because in the end, it was Li who would be trapped and alone. I wanted to take him with me, take him out into the world and save him like he had saved me. But I wanted it all. I wanted to save this world, too, and I knew they could not coexist.

I draped my paper wings over my shoulders like a cape, stretching and feeling them root into me like feathered tendons. *Feeling* them. They really were a part of me, spreading outwards and furling in, testing the air before I took off. It was a short flight; I scattered a few paper cranes from a chandelier, catching the chain in one hand as I landed. I let it sway beneath me as I surveyed the country the library had become.

The walls were no longer distinct; they were just the idea of walls, stretching out infinite on every side into different places; Asgard there, Robert Service's Yukon there. Baker Street, Shangri-La. And the places flexed in the same way my wings did, shifting like an aurora shooting through a prism, warping into whatever we saw fit for it to be. The library was breathing; it had come alive in our care alone, and I could feel that it wouldn't let me go so easily.

I hoped that it wouldn't.

Whistle whistle.

I turned. Li waxed casual on another chandelier across the room. When he got my attention, he waggled his fingers in a greeting, flitting his own pair of dragonfly wings out as he grabbed hold of his chandelier's chain and rocked back and forth. He was turning his fixture into a swing.

"Hey!" I called, using every ounce of my will not to copy him. "I need to talk to you."

The arc of his chandelier grew wider and wider. Once he got something like this into his head, there was no stopping him, so I might as well play along. I climbed up the chain, wrapping my feet and hands around it and leaning, plunging my body back and forth, using my wings to push until the heavy *whoosh* of our chandeliers matched. With every upswing they came closer together, foot by foot, but our eyes never left each other, daring, challenging. I felt a slight drop and, looking up, saw that both of our chains were working away from the ceiling. Li had noticed, too. This was going to go off with a bang for sure. *3 . . . 2 . . . 1 . . .*

We leapt off in unison, flashing into the air just as the chandeliers broke free of their moorings and slammed into one another, exploding in a supernova of glass and light. Li caught me perfectly in his arms inside the firework wake of our beautiful explosion, the glass turning into shooting stars around us. Just another day, another miracle. But today his eyes, the ones I always so easily fell into, held me like a butterfly in a bell jar. It was the way I always dreamed someone might look at me; not only look, but see. I let them trap me under glass. It was where I wanted to be.

He brought us down onto the carved banister of one of the landings. The usual dark now flickered with tiny globes of light that had beaded off our chandeliers to float around us like fireflies.

Li dusted me off perfunctorily before hurrying me through the stacks and towards our secret place.

"Okay, okay," I said, trying to pry my hand out of his and get down to business as he bustled me through the door. The room was still filled with the artificial sunlight of the poems we had been sharing that morning, the ground as soft and spongy as a spring meadow. I called it our Terrarium Room, and it was only growing thicker with paper flowers the more time we spent there. Li sat me down on our sofa and shook himself like an overwrought dog, his wings exploding into a hundred swallows that shot off into the fireplace. I simply folded mine tight to my back, watching him rock back and forth on his heels, impatient with himself. He went through the motions of shrugging his coat off, of fiddling with his hands, of trying to find a comfortable place to stand. He had something on his mind, too.

"Oh, sit down," I teased, feigning the casual air as questions and mostly apologies tumbled in my stomach like a rinse cycle.

He came and sat carefully next to me, and even just feeling

the weight of him beside me made my throat constrict. I was nervous. How could I do this? I had to focus; we could work this out together. I looked down at my hands, searching them for the words to tell him that this was all going to be over soon. And that I wanted to be with him. That this went beyond friendship. That I—

I felt his shoulder press against me as he reached up and tapped my nose affectionately, disarming my anxiety with that trademark smile. His mouth was so close to mine, and his eyes would not let go. This time, I didn't push him away. I would have pulled him closer if my hands weren't clenching each other in my lap.

He took them in his, lifting them up, and in parting them he produced one of my Polaroids. Then he reached out and popped one from behind my ear, from out of my nose. He was trying to cheer me up, but it only made it worse.

"This is serious," I finally said, stopping the magic show as the pictures scattered to the floor. "Listen. Li, I . . ." I winced my eyes shut, trying to concentrate. "This can't last."

When I opened my eyes again, all I could see was his Adam's apple rise and fall at his throat, his smile turning down faster than I could let the words spill out. He let go of my hands.

"No!" I tried to recover. "Li, it's not you. It's not me, either. Please hear me out. I would . . . give *anything* to stay here with you. But the summer is nearly over and I . . . and . . ."

Despite the colour draining from him, he let his eyebrows shoot up, demanding that I just say it.

"I'm leaving."

The rustling of paper wings. From the corner of my eye I

saw the slow shower of crumpled pages floating to the ground
in the shadows of the fireplace, a paper bird dying with every
heartbeat. Li's eyes went elsewhere, and our terrarium started
fading.

I couldn't do it. Not to him. Not for the world. I caved in,
my head dropping to his chest to find reassurance there. Our
world was going to break apart. I couldn't be the cause of it.

"But I don't want to," I whimpered, body shaking. I felt the
ghost of his hands hovering over me, too stunned to hold me.
I instantly got to my feet, trying to hide my face in my hands
and keep him at my back, pacing and holding my head steady
as I clenched the sobs back with my teeth.

"It's all going to end," I said, partway frantic. "And where
will we be when it does? They're tearing this place down,
they're taking me away . . . but I can't, I can't. This is my
home. Whatever it is, wherever it is. My home is with *you.*"

It blurted out of me and I felt relief, felt like I was releasing
something that had been nurtured in the dark. And he was
behind me, encircling my body with his arms and pulling me
close. I could smell musty pages, the spice of his skin, and
almost the tangibility of his heart. Almost.

"I don't want to leave," I whispered again, wanting to fall
into him.

He put his head on my shoulder and turned me so I was
looking up at him, so he could bend down to my cheeks and
kiss the tears away. *You don't have to,* I swore I heard as his lips
grazed near mine.

And then our mouths touched fully, like two palms praying
together. Praying for the miracle we needed. Warmth rushed
up and through me like a comet. He held me tight.

And my phone went off.

I had made a point this morning of turning it off, but Mum must have nabbed it and made sure it was at high volume before I left. I pulled away from Li and yanked it out of my pocket, hanging it up with the smash of a button. It sprang to life again, no matter what I did, and though tempted to pitch it across the room, I stopped myself. I looked at Li and stretched my wings once, letting them coalesce into a swirling storm of moths at my back.

"I have to tell her," I said, the words that might have once been alien now entirely my own. "I have to end this. I'll be back soon, I promise."

I went for the door, but he made a sudden grab for my hand. This time there was no worry that I wouldn't return. We were bound by a golden thread that not even Fate could cut.

"I promise," I repeated.

Promises, promises. They were all I had left to give, and as I left the library for the last time before returning to it forever, I promised that Treade would get no more from me.

· ○ ● ○ ●

It was dark. How could it have gotten so dark, so quickly? I didn't remember being in the library that long, and hadn't I left with the morning sun at my back? Everything was getting away from me, especially the fight; I was already losing it as I crept into the kitchen, the burning tip of Mum's lit cigarette the only light on in the house.

"Do you know what time it is?" There was no jagged joke behind the question, snappish and irate. Only the venom that she'd been shooting at me for weeks now. As my eyes rolled into my head to find the answer, she was more than willing to speak for me. "It's nearly *midnight*, Ashleigh!"

I somehow found this hard to believe, despite how dark it was out, or how the digital clock on the microwave gave stark evidence to her cause. I shook my head to retaliate. "So? It's the summer. I'm a teenager. Maybe if you went out sometime and got a life of your own, you'd stop thinking about me." I darted out of the kitchen and up the stairs to my room. I had to get out of here.

"I'm talking to you, Ashleigh!" she shouted, chasing after me. "What are you doing?"

I was shoving clothes and essentials into my bag, primed for flight, even with my wings left behind at the library. "I'm doing what you've been hounding me to do for the last month. I'm packing."

"Ashleigh, if you'd just tell me what this was about— Where are you *going*?"

"Away. I'm going away." *Come away, O human child! / To the waters and the wild / With a faery, hand in hand, / For the world's more full of weeping than you can understand.* I could hear the water rising, a great wave recoiling like a boa constrictor. I had to hurry. I rushed past her but she grabbed me by the sleeve and held tight.

"Ashleigh, this has to stop. What's going on? Are you in some kind of trouble? Please, just talk to me. This isn't like you."

I yanked free, seeing right through her. "No." A voice came out of the water and took mine over. "This is exactly me. I have to get away from all of you. From this place. It's been stifling me all along. But I found someplace better, somewhere I can be free. Where I can do anything."

I felt the medallion that Li had given me start to turn hot against my neck, almost burning, alive. These words weren't mine. At the library I had been clear-headed, had known that I was going to tell my mother everything, to make her understand. But now I was consumed, transformed into someone else who would protect this secret at any cost. My mother looked like a stranger to me, and I could see the feeling was mutual as she backed up a step and let me pass. I caught the glint in my eye in the hall mirror. There was absolutely nothing left of that guilt or disapproval in them. It had all been replaced with a determined fury, an angry resolution I barely knew. I was suddenly aware of my skin, of every hair standing on edge, and I knew that I would not be consumed by the wave coming for me. I would ride it out of here instead.

They have been holding me back all along. But I could do great things now. I could make the world and unmake it. And here and now, I could shed it.

I felt my mother's hand on my shoulder. "Ashleigh, please. Just talk to me."

I felt myself whirl around, felt my hands lunge out and push her away, but it wasn't me. It was the wave. Caught unaware, she sidestepped and tripped halfway down the stairs. She landed and choked, wind knocked out of her. Then she started coughing.

The sound raked up and down my ears, and suddenly I felt the buzz of being awake, eyes snapping into focus like someone who had just fallen out of bed. I looked down at Mum, crouched on the floor, coughing and coughing, and I froze. The coughing turned to desperate gasping as she pressed her hands down on her chest and her face darkened in the shadows of the hallway.

I flew down beside her, unable to calm her. Her body suddenly went slack and still. "Mum? *Mum?*"

I dialled 9-1-1 frantically. In the intervening minutes as I waited numbly for the ambulance, the wave pulled back from the shore. Like it had never been there at all.

Unable to sleep, she watches the patterns of light cast onto the ceiling by the sun and trees dancing there. Her journal lays open on top of her weak legs, but she cannot bring herself to sit up and scrawl in it, despite doctor's orders. She has managed to write *bad day* across the page in wilted script, pen abandoned at her side. Her breathing is shallow, each intake and exhale a trial, and she swears she can feel her heart valves failing beneath her chest. She berates herself for this insidious weakness, for every single moment it has stolen from the life she wanted to lead. She nearly lost her son because of it (birth had been made difficult enough by her constant illness), and she has lost so much more in spite of surviving even that ordeal. On days like these, delirious from the combination of dizziness and the large measures of digoxin she has been administered, she is certain that the dim outline of her husband sits at her bedside, watching her with hooded eyes and disappointment. She was supposed to live for both of them, but she can't even do this for herself.

"Don't look at me like that," she hisses at the ghost.

". . . in her room," someone says in the hallway, her hearing swinging in and out of focus, unsure if she really heard the front door slamming, or footsteps pattering closer.

The effort it takes her to turn her head is like parting a sea. The ghost of her husband has moved, inhabiting the haunted, drawn face of her son in the doorway.

"Mama," he says, pulling up a chair at her bedside and clasping her swollen hand in his, warm with life. "You just couldn't wait to collapse until *after* I came back from Winnipeg, could you?"

She cracks her first smile in hours, finding relief just in reaching up and touching his face. "Sorry about that. I was getting impatient."

As a racking cough takes her over, Ruth floats through the door, bearing a basin with cool water and a washcloth. "It happened just as she was getting up, no real warning," she croons in her

French-Canadian patois. "The doctor has been and gone, says she needs at least a week's rest to recover from the episode."

From beneath the cough, the patient finds a laugh. "A week's rest is what will kill me, not this failing heart of mine."

Her son helps her to sit up, despite Ruth's protestations to rest and recover. He politely bids her to leave the basin, and the two of them, alone.

Removing his jacket and rolling up his sleeves, he dips the washcloth in the basin, wrings it out, and rests it against her forehead. She shuts her eyes, refreshing coolness washing over her. "How are you feeling now?" he asks.

She drags her eyelids open and sighs. "Like a foolish child. I should be the one taking care of you."

"You take well enough care of me; just work on yourself for a change." He takes his seat again and reaches for her journal, leafing through it and smiling approvingly. "I see your journal entries are deviating from the purely medical ones the doctor prescribed."

"Don't you know it's rude to read a lady's diary?" She turns to him. "Besides, the way I approach this new life of ours is tantamount to my recovery. Writing 'good day because I had a bowel movement' doesn't really make it a good day. Doctor Buren thinks far too linearly for his own good or mine."

He has stopped on a particular page, brow furrowed as he dissects a drawing she had made last week. He flips it over so she can see. "And what's this?"

Her heavy eyes fall down upon it. "Don't you recognize it? It's your library idea."

It is a crude sketch of a three-storey building, followed by a floor plan and various ideas scribbled in the margins. Flipping the pages, he scans the notes and blinks up at her. "I wouldn't have thought you'd take that idea so seriously."

She reaches up to dab the washcloth beneath her jaw and down her neck, spirits improving, little by little. "I thought it could be a project we might oversee together. Make us feel a little more at home here. Keep us . . . distracted."

He exhales through his mouth, placing the silver-plated journal on her nightstand. His face is slack and exhausted. "I'd rather you just focus on getting better. We can think about it next spring."

"Next spring . . ." she trails off. She does not think she will last until then. "I don't want to wait, Nel. This will do us some good. It will do this town some good, in return for all it has done for us. Besides, the locals could use a decent library. Something to distract them from their common rural activities."

He pats her head. "Such a romantic." Fishing around in his coat pocket, he produces his beaten copy of Coleridge. "Would you like me to read to you a little, or would you like to sleep?"

"*I'm* the romantic?" she evades, pointing at the book. "You weren't at a Grain Exchange summit at all, I bet. You were out wooing, again." It was his common practice to carry poetry, and being caught reading it in his spare time had drawn many a lady into the web of his charm, from both the city and Treade. The son of a business tycoon as the paragon of the wandering dreamer magnetised any girl in the province, but he had always been particular, and she never intervened in his affairs of the heart, for she understood it as sacred ground.

He flushes, ruffling his hair and turning the pages of his anthology. "I don't know if I'll ever find my Genevieve." He stares into the distance, beyond the book. "Or have a great love, like you did."

She regards her son sadly. He does not often speak with compliment on the subject of his father, so she takes this as an opportunity to underscore it with something encouraging. "It doesn't take great people to create great love," she takes his hand.

"Love is fleeting and it comes at a cost, and it often ends so quickly you don't have the time to recognize it when it's in your hands." She shuts her eyes, thinking of all the arguments she and David had before the end, how deeply his work furrowed into his soul and replaced his family, even his love for her. But beneath it, she knew all of it had been for them, his intentions and his love sorely skewed but still just at the surface. She thinks of how she felt in his arms, how, to her soul, she trusted him while he encircled her.

"I loved your father," she blurts, reeling herself back in. "Don't you ever believe that I didn't."

He is stunned. "Mother, I—"

"I loved him more than my body could bear, that's how it feels sometimes, when I get like this." She looks at her son with an intensity that surpasses her exhaustion, and silences any more of his protests. "He did not make it easy to love him, sometimes. But any kind of love, even the kind that hurts you, is a miracle. And you, my love? *You* will love so greatly that it will change the fabric of the world around you. Your love will not be a miracle. It will *make* miracles."

She eases back into her pillows, sighing and closing her eyes, relief washing over her. "And I wish with what little heart I have left that I get to be there when it happens for you."

His grey eyes shine. "Don't give up on me yet," he whispers. "This story isn't over."

No, not yet, she thinks. Because when that happens she will be able to rest, really rest. And dream again.

DATE
ISSUED TO
CHAPTER THIRTEEN
PROPERTY OF
TREADE
PUBLIC LIBRARY

My hearing kept swinging in and out. I could almost feel my eardrums dilating wide when the doctor said she'd be all right, then feel them closing up again as soon as words like *severe emphysema, chronic pneumonia*, or *possible lung transplant* came anywhere near me. All sounds were suspended in the rushing water long before they could hurt me.

The doctor leaned in to ascertain if I was listening, his glasses flashing in the antiseptic fluorescents of Treade General. "We're going to keep her overnight, okay? We need to do a full ultrasound in the morning to determine how extensive her condition is, and she'll be put on oxygen and low-level bronchodilators for most of the night." His words were far away. I looked up at him, just for a second, in case it might help me understand. It wasn't just my hearing that was going, it seemed. It was my eyes, too; his features were swimming around on his skull, flesh rippling and blurring like a churned lake, until he really didn't have a face at all. None of them did, not the nurses who were checking Mum's IV drip, not the orderlies passing by in the hall. So I just looked at Mum and nodded at everything he said, whatever it was he was saying, willing him to go away like you would a nightmare.

I tensed as his hand found my shoulder. "You should go home and get some rest," he said. *Nod nod.* He finally left us alone and I breathed a little easier.

I couldn't stop staring at Mum. She looked so small, like her skin was too tight on her bones. Why hadn't I noticed that before? And there were lines on her eyes and mouth that hadn't been there. Even sleeping she looked sad and frustrated, forehead creased as she tried to work through the riddle of the poison in her lungs. Or the riddle of me. Of how I could be fading away from her into some other place so quickly and so willingly.

She swam in and out of focus, and I had a hard time pinpointing her on the hospital bed in front of me. There was something else going on here. I couldn't see reality in the same way anymore, couldn't experience it like everyone else. My perception had been cut open and altered, and it wasn't just happening in the library now. It was inside me, a briar patch of thorns tangled around my insides and clenching, and whatever it was, it wouldn't let me stay here in the real world. This parasite could only survive inside the dream, and it was looking to me to save it. So it was doing the only natural thing it could: it was calling me back to the one place I could feel safe. And I was willing to follow it.

The lights flickered so hard they became strobes. I couldn't take my eyes off Mum's still body, couldn't stop experiencing a gut-wrenching squall of guilt and the hunger to run. But then her face started to blend on itself, started to become an unrecognizable slate, and I knew that this was it. I started backing away into the hall. Nurses blurred past me, faceless. I couldn't handle this place, this harsh, frail landscape where nothing could be controlled, where I couldn't will it to assert itself into a new shape, a new dream. My mother was my last anchor to the world, and she was too weak to keep it pinned down anymore.

So even if it was just for a moment, a few seconds, I needed my dream; I was feverish for it. The briar patch inside me stretched, sending thorny tendrils down my nerve endings and up my spine. They made me walk out of the hospital, climb onto a bus, and ride away from there, and I let their barbs do their work so long as it would get me back to where I belonged. They made me get off the bus and walked me in a trance, letting go of my puppet strings once I reached Wilson's Woods. In the distance, silhouetted against the prairie night, was the library.

My phone went off, but instead of the usual ring tone, all I could hear was a horrible screeching, underpinned by a high-frequency pinging. I cried out, throwing myself to the ground and covering my ears. They had become so used to hearing everything on a submerged, low volume that this sound, breaking through the water, made them feel like they were bleeding. I tore through my bag to find my phone, find the screaming beacon that would call me back to Treade and keep me from what I wanted.

Tabitha calling.

I smashed it against a rock, shattering the teeth-grinding sound and the glass display without a second thought. Blissful silence prevailed. Nothing or no one would stop me now. I got up, shaking, and with a renewed calm at what seemed like a small victory, I picked up the pace towards sanctuary.

There was music wafting out of my porthole, and light. Soft, remarkable light. I squeezed through and stood up, listening. *Moon river* . . . It carried me, this beautiful song, past our infinite shelves, past our aurora portals that crossed into other worlds, until I stood beneath our brilliant paper sky. The result of our chandelier supernova hung as twinkling shards in the air, and it felt like I was walking through a garden of stars. The library was awash in its usual orange glow, the kind that tried to convince us it was sunlight, but this was the only light I needed. Would ever need. I stood in the centre of the room, shut my eyes, and waited.

The shelves moved back, receding and becoming part of the shifting walls. The tables, the chairs, the chandeliers, the deer clock. It all faded back and away. The ground undulated under me, but I rode it like a breaker and kept my balance. I held my breath. And when I opened my eyes, there was only night, and cavern walls, and so many stars, and Li.

And Xanadu.

The thorns around me loosened. Now they would bow to my will, just as this place had. I breathed, free, and Li touched my face, eyes dancing, fingers finding my pulse and resting there, drinking it in. He put his arms around me and we swayed, my skin coming alive in the shard-dotted darkness, my soul flexing and taking flight past sinuous rills, sunny domes, caves of ice. Paradise. The last thought I had before giving my entire self up to it was of my mother, receding in her hospital bed into the shadow of a world I wasn't a part of anymore. And I started crying, even as I forgot her and everything else that used to be important to me.

Li's hands clenched me close, flattening me against him as we swayed to the sound of a dulcimer being plucked in the distance. I was sobbing, but his hands soothed me. *You're home now*, they said, patting my hair and sighing.

"I know," I replied.

He gently moved my body away from his, lake eyes pooling with whorls and tendrils of fog. A phantom smile passed his mouth, and the veins of his dragonfly wings flickered into view. They were no longer made of paper; they shone like translucent holographic foil and buzzed hypnotically against the dark. As though I were one of his paper birds, he plucked me from the floor, and we lifted into the air, climbing out of the underground cavern and into our sea of stars, until we were enveloped by green. An ancient garden that stretched to infinity on either side greeted us, just at the brink of twilight. This dream of a poem was our dream now. And we climbed higher and higher over it, the music and the river Alph meandering in our wake.

We were in our Terrarium Room. Even though it looked nothing like it had when I first saw it, devoid now of the sofa, the giant fireplace aviary, the hardwood, the walls. There was none of that now; only a patch of green interspersed with saplings, water trickling nearby. It was our secluded place, where we could be quiet and be at peace and really take in one another.

Li placed me tenderly on the ground. Night fell in full around us, pinpricked only by firefly stars. We stood side by side, enraptured by the glory of what we could make just by shutting our eyes, kicking our hearts into gear, and imagining. We could stay here forever. We could disappear here.

His arms encircled my waist, hands brushing like gentle hummingbirds against my rib cage. I craned my neck to look up at him, just to see his eyes before it all happened. I begged whatever power we had to let him speak, let him say the words, let what I felt be real without just having to trust that his intentions are pure. He kissed me, fully, gently, then his lips trailed down to my neck and pulled me towards him, pulled me down, and his hands had stopped feeling comforting, had stopped saying, *you're home.*

Now they said, *you're mine.*

· ∘ ● ∘ ●

There was just the dream now.

Time passed in currents. I couldn't tell if it had been ten minutes or ten days, and at first, I revelled in it. What else was there to do but trounce from story to story, dream to dream, Li close at hand? Had there ever been anything besides this? I felt like the words on the pages were being tattooed under my skin, rising to the surface when I called them. And I could call them whenever I so wished. We were nearing godhood, and this was our incubus. We could do anything, we could shape words and worlds and shape ourselves, too.

And I revelled in it. For a time.

After countless masquerades, night flights to Venus, trips to the halls of Odin and back again, I could feel something shifting in me. It started as a sort of insistence, as an itch. Sometimes I would catch myself staring off into the distance of wherever we were, whether it was Lilliput or Mount Olympus, and I would feel it. A hair in my eye, a stitch in my side, a tickle in my throat. A half sneeze. I ignored it, telling my body to simply adjust to whatever was growing in the pit of my stomach. And sometimes, out of the blue, I would feel a chill, infiltrating my pores even when we stood in the desert of Arabia or under the Caribbean sun. That was how it started.

Then these feelings went away, and for a while I felt like I had finally grown into my own in this world, that I was accepted into the fold. But the feelings hadn't gone away, they were just changing tack. The stitches in my side or the hair in my eye became someone tapping me on the shoulder, someone whispering in my ear. At moments like this I would turn to Li and see him watching me expectantly, his forehead furrowed. I asked him if he had heard anything, but he only smiled, coming close and touching the medallion that still hung around my neck, growing heavier every moment. *I'll protect you*, said the gesture. I had become adept at reading him without having to guess what he was thinking, or to speak as often as before. We could read each other without words, something he was pleased I could do, and I knew for certain that his next smile said, *you're imagining things* and *stop worrying and enjoy yourself.* So I ignored it, ignored the feeling that there was something I was missing, something I had forgotten.

But the whispering, the tugging . . . it grew. My brow would furrow like I was trying to remember a certain word on the tip of my tongue, trying to puzzle out what I was hearing. Trying to remember words.

I stopped in the middle of climbing a great hill made out of viney tendrils, and when Li realized I wasn't following him, he looked down at me, confused.

"Don't you hear it?" I said, looking off into the distance, way-pointing every detail of the jungle we were picnicking in. "There's something I'm . . . forgetting . . ."

The confines of this world, this story, shifted, the sky and the trees rippling like I was seeing them through the inside of an aquarium. For a second I thought I saw the library on the other side. I kept my eyes on it . . .

Li's cold grip on my wrist snapped me out of my daze, and the jungle reasserted its solidity. When our eyes met, I was shocked by the firm discontent in his stare. He shook his head and dragged me along.

I didn't sleep. I didn't eat. I didn't need to, just like Li. We were being fed, in a way, and we would shut our eyes for a time, retreat to the library for a change of scenery only, but these moments were few and far between. Getting a moment to myself was impossible, because Li was my shadow, always watching, always in the wake of my steps. And while I was distracted in some adventure we had concocted, Li was changing the library behind my back. The window in our Terrarium Room had been swallowed, and for the longest time I couldn't tell if I had imagined it even being there in the first place. The petals of the rose window were just a painting, now. It was just walls and books and stories and shadows. And I was fine with that. As soon as it was changed, I only smiled, assuming it had always been that way. There was just the library. It kept us safe.

But Li wouldn't let us stay there for long. Just as I was getting settled into familiar territory, Li was bidding me to get up, to help him build another word country and trounce off. But my physical body was weak without nourishment, and even though he was doing everything to feed my senses, it wasn't enough.

"I'm tired," I'd say. But he would level me with that same stare, like I was being an obstinate, disobedient child. He was so persistent that we stay enveloped in these dreams longer and longer. When I let them fall apart from simply being worn out, he would scold me with a harsher tone of silence than I had known him to give.

"Please don't look at me like that. I'm not doing it on purpose. I just don't—"

He would put his hand over my mouth and shake his head again, pulling me close, running a hand over my hair as he kissed and kissed it. *No words now. Hush. You don't need them. Don't worry, you'll get used to this.*

Sometimes we would lie together in the quiet, testing each other's bodies like iridescent puddles. He would lie behind me, arms holding me tight and fitting the curve of my spine perfectly against him. He wanted us to occupy the same space, and that need radiated into me, and I did my best to open myself up to him. His breath was shallow, and unnaturally cold, against my alert nape. He was trying to name each strand of my hair, memorizing my shape, and owning me little by little. I turned over in his hands to face him, his finger stroking the pulse beat at my throat. There was that smile again. *It's getting easier*, it said. *It won't be long now.* He pressed his ghost lips to mine.

The whispering died away.

· ○ ● ○ ●

And then there was the water.

It did not come in a rush or a wave, did not drown everything out like it once did. It merely haunted my steps; things sounded wet, looked wet. And the whispering came back the closer I was to it; a lake, a river, the sea. I felt like I could let the water swallow me and bear me away, but I was afraid of this feeling. And water became suddenly prevalent in every story we dove into, even though I tried to resist, tried to will it to become something else, something stable. But Li only smiled and reached out for my hand, and all I could do was trust.

We were in Shalott. It felt far more familiar than it should have, considering we had never been there before. I was the lady, melancholy on my barge filled with tapestries and possessions. Li was my Lancelot, riding alongside my boat as it cruised down the river towards its end. The sun felt so real against my pale skin, and I basked in it as Li watched me from his gleaming-white steed, eyes trained on every shift of muscle under my flesh. It felt like he was expecting something to happen here, some end that both of us had been working towards.

I ignored him and turned away, sitting at the prow, looking out into the distance. The sky had turned to lead. There was the dark promise of a storm haunting the air, a demonic mobile over the baby's crib as the infant shied away. It was quiet for the first time, and the water was calm as glass. It did not bring up any fear in me, and I leaned over the edge, letting my hand skim the surface. This was peace, and I embraced it. I looked down into the black water, and lost myself there.

The whispering rocketed into my head like a heavy moth battering inside my skull.

"*Listen,*" it said.

I prickled but didn't move, didn't give anything away. I glanced at Li. His horse was nickering and shying, trying to pull away from the river. The boat was moving slower now as it made its way to Camelot, and when I looked ahead, I saw a single house coming into view on the horizon. I suddenly remembered how this poem ended, and my heart clenched. But the whispering grew into a hum, one voice overlapping again and again, like a wave hushing against a rock. And I strained to hear.

"*Closer,*" it said. "*Closer.*"

Something was moving under the water, rising from the riverbed. I leaned nearer to the surface, ear first, eyes locked onto Li's. He was trying to control his horse, but his face was stricken, because he knew I had heard the question, knew that he couldn't get to me in time:

"*What's your name?*" said the water voice.

"My . . ." I tried to repeat the words, but I had forgotten them. Forgotten everything.

Then a hand that had haunted even my waking dreams broke the glass surface and grabbed hold of my medallion, yanking me off the boat, dragging me down into somewhere else.

. ○ ● ○ ●

I am looking out at the crashing waters of Lake Jovan, churning with absolution like they never have before. The wind weeps for me, weeps for itself, and forces me to look on. A sick throb pulses in my belly through my torn cotton dress, clinging with sheet rain to my shaking skin. The cold has me in its grip and confiscates what little warmth has been keeping my heart beating. I'm not alone. I see her standing on the precipice, looking at the water along with me. She turns her sad, watery eyes to me.

"He is trying to take your name from you so he can keep you with him forever," she whispers, but her mouth doesn't move. "He lost his own name, and it is what has trapped him here. Protect your name. Protect your story. Listen. Listen." The voice was rising, desperate. "What's your *name?*"

I stumble, falling backwards into empty space, into a purling blackness. She turns back to the water, watching. Waiting.

· ○ ● ○ ●

I hit the hardwood of the library floor with an urgency that sends a jolt up my spine. Wind knocked out of me, I watched the edges of Shalott scatter across the ceiling like frightened water striders, crackling away as the shelves and the walls came back into their own. Li was at my side, trying to get me to stand, and all of a sudden something struck me like I was a hollow bell. I lunged away from him.

". . . my name!" I heard myself blurt. The sound of any speech at all seemed foreign, since we had grown accustomed to not speaking, only reading each other. I needed words now, though, so I repeated again and again. "My name. My *name.*"

I was shaking, muttering under my breath. *How could I have forgotten it? How?* He took both of my hands and pressed them to his chest, trying to comfort me.

"Don't!" I ripped them away and stalked off, pacing. "How could I forget it? I mean. I've always had one. I've always been . . ."

My mind flashed back to the lake I'd only just dreamed of, to the woman. She was looking at me with the same kind of expectation Li had been grinding into me.

"I'm . . ."

Smoke, tea, a hospital bed. The sun glinting over trees. A house. A canvas.

And a library.

"I'm Ash."

I suddenly remembered Li and our first meeting, in the library back when I had first seen it, diminished and dark in the eye of a rainstorm. I remembered Li looking down at my proffered hand and how he had whitened. Because I knew his name had been taken from him, too. Until I had given it back.

"I'm Ash," I repeated, jolting back into the here and now. I slowly turned around to face Li, his eyes a pair of overcast funnel clouds. He reached out a hand to me but I shied away from it, raising a hand to my head as every memory pounded fresh into my cortex. My eyes felt bleary, like I had been asleep for too long.

"God," I muttered. "What time is it? What . . ." I looked around, instinct kicking in to find a window, find the sun. "What *day* is it? Li? How long have I been here with you?"

He kept trying to gather me close to him, to mend the seam between us that was slowly starting to pop apart. But I was having none of it.

"No, don't." I backed away, woozy and panting as I was caught up in the net of his worried face. "Please, I . . . Oh, God. Mum. *Mum.*"

I broke into a panicked sob, remembering her in her hospital bed, looking so small and vulnerable. And I had left her there alone. "Is she okay? Is she still sick? Oh, God, I don't even remember leaving the hospital." I whirled around, trying to find my bag, racing and weaving around the shelves. "Help me find it, okay? My bag. I need my bag," I said over my shoulder, trying to keep it together even though I was so light-headed. He followed heavily in my footsteps, almost at a prowl. I stopped, overcome, leaning against one of the inset shelves and trying to catch my breath. I pressed my palm deep into my forehead. I wanted to throw up and pass out all at once, but I had to get to my phone. My phone . . .

"Maybe it's upstairs, in our room—" I spun into the aisle, nearly falling over myself. Li caught me and steadied me. "Thanks," I sighed, grateful. "I feel so strange . . ."

I tried pulling away towards the stairs, but he wouldn't let go. He knew I was trying to leave.

"What is it?"

His eyes were becoming as dark as pools of ink. Beyond him, I could see reams and reams of pages floating down from the ceiling, the shelves. Our sky was unfolding on itself, our birds and creatures limp. There was so much paper raining down that I couldn't focus on Li. But he shook me, hard and impatiently.

"*What?*" I snapped, pushing him away. His fists clenched and unclenched at his sides as he fought with his inability to communicate, his frustration that I could no longer read and understand him. I slipped around him, towards the stairs. "My mother, she's sick and I . . ." I shook my head, trying to escape his stare. "I have to go."

He clattered up the stairs behind me, and I tried to walk faster, tried to shake him. I couldn't stand him so close to me right now, not when he was acting like this. The floor-boards groaned under my feet, and I suddenly felt claustro-phobic surrounded by shelves. At the top of the stairs he grabbed me again.

"Stop it, Li, I'm serious." He pulled me to him, tried to cap-ture me in an embrace, but I prickled. "I don't have time for this!" I snapped again, suddenly afraid of his urgency and des-peration to keep me close. Something gleamed in the corner of my eye: water was beading out of the bookshelves, dripping.

I pushed back. "Please, just let me go." His forearms tightened around me like I was cutting him each time I tried to
get away. "I'll . . . I'll come back," I lied. "I promise I will."
He shook his head, not believing me for a second. I pried his
hands off. "I have to," I whispered firmly, the weight of the
words giving me the strength to move away.

In a sudden turn he nabbed me by the shoulders and
checked me into the banister of the landing, pinning me
there. The carved wood rail dug an angry groove into my
spine. I cried out. "What are you—"

He took my face between his hands, searching it, the grimace at his mouth reeling back as he tried to take us into a
story, a dream, just so he could shackle me down to him and
the library, to make me accept whatever my fate would be. I
could feel it closing in, but I shouted, "No! I don't want this,
not this way." The dream hissed backwards like a feral beast,
receding into the walls. Water was cascading down them,
creeping towards our feet. I still had some power here, even
though it was quickly ebbing away.

His mouth quivered, pushing back tears. He didn't want
me to leave, but he didn't want to force me to stay either.
How could I help but want to get away, afraid as I was in his
hands, instantly forgetting all the playful and tender ways he
had held me before? His grip faltered and he dipped his forehead, pressing it into mine. *Please*, his hands muttered over
my cheeks. *Please don't leave me here.*

I couldn't look at him as I offered him the lie a second time.
"I'll come back," I quavered. "But you have to let me go."

His fingers ground into my shoulders as he lifted his eyes
to me. They were black pearls, unforgiving, as the only word
I had ever heard Li speak was snarled into my face: "*No.*"

Something went off, and everything slowed to a mercurial pace. I saw everything unfold piece by piece as it all fell into place, until time caught up with me and crashed against my frail human body in one fell swoop. First, the shelves creaked backwards, smashing into one another like a steady stream of dominoes, upending from one end of the library to the other. Books on the wall shelves poured free of their moorings and fell in a waterfall to the ground, forced out of the wall by geysers of exploding water behind them. It pooled down the walls and cracked the shelves open, floor heaving up to meet the splintered wood. The water was as black as Li's eyes, as unrelenting, and it rose higher with every half tick of my pulse. It took an age to look back at Li as I felt his hands kneading into my flesh, lifting me bodily from the floor and over the banister.

Time pressed itself back together in a guttural *snap*.

"Li—"

He shook his head and did like I asked — he *let me go*.

My heart was a raging powder keg, now. Plummeting towards the floor, the first thought that gripped me was that this couldn't be it. The sense of reason I had abandoned came to my rescue, full tilt — *I had power here once before. Use it.*

I winced my eyes shut.

I opened them.

The torrent of birds rushed behind me, and though I only had energy to generate momentary wings, it was enough. They flared wide and pushed, and they were the difference between the life I still wanted and the one that Li thought could make us both happy. I paused before making impact with the floor, and I saw Li leaning over the banister, eyes clear and horrified, whatever had overtaken him having fled now that its work was complete. He reached out for me but betrayal bloomed in my blood. Damage done.

A hurling fist of water leapt out of the wall and dragged me down. It wasn't deep enough yet to submerge me totally, and I sprang from the floor back to the surface. The library lights were guttering and buzzing, one after another exploding under the weight of the water that burst from the wall behind them. The noise was thunderous, and the walls creaked, threatening at any moment to come undone under the pressure. The deer clock tumbled off the wall and sank. The spiral staircases heaved, shuddered, and collapsed in on themselves like Slinkies. I couldn't tell if this was just another one of Li's constructions; either this was his reaction to my leaving, or his final, desperate means of keeping me here. The water was chest deep. I ploughed past piles of books and busted shelves, trying to find my porthole out of here.

A tremor heaved the room, but I persisted to the familiar wall that had always taken me out and in. It was growing too dark and the water too deep to see it, so I dove. I patted the wall, but there was no hole, no inconsistencies, nothing. My exit, like the windows and the outside world, had been blocked off and hidden by Li. This was his last resort.

I resurfaced. "Li!" I screamed over the din of the deluge brewing inside the once-sacred palace. "I can't stay here, you know I can't! Please, just help me *stop this*."

I couldn't wade anymore, so I swam; swam to the place where the rose window had once been, skirting past and using shelves as push-off points. There was so much debris jutting out of the water, and the darkness was almost entire — something caught my ankle and splashed me forward. I lurched up to catch my breath after swallowing a mouthful of bitter lake water, and I realized Li's medallion was caught on something. In a moment of panic, I yanked my head back, desperate to free myself, and the chain snapped. I scrambled to catch it, but it slipped away.

I looked up to the place where the rose window should have been. The painting of the window that stood in its place was an immaculate deception, another perfect *trompe l'oeil*, and I glared at it, hoping that the anxious panic I felt could turn it back to glass. Nothing. I couldn't even summon my wings back to buy some time, let alone muster the window. I could make worlds, and here was another one, unravelling around me. I looked and looked and looked for the way out, begged Li to help me, to save me this one last time. But he was gone.

Then I saw the Fable Door, carvings etched in obsidian shadow and the few guttering lights that were defiantly left. I surged towards it, water reaching to my neck now and the floor slipping away from my toes. I kicked and stroked until I was pressing my body against the wood, grasping the handles with everything, yanking and twisting. I dove under, tried to see if there was something I was missing. There was a keyhole, wide and gaping, and I pressed my eye to it. I could see outside, precious, beautiful outside. The dawn was climbing up the collar of Wilson's Woods. I tried the handle again but it snapped free. For an instant, I was more focused on the door itself; underwater, the carvings were alive, surging like frightened minnows and staring at me like I was *their* nightmare. They didn't want this either. They just kept swimming up.

I surfaced, gasping, choking. I slapped my hands furiously against the door. There were no options now. I pressed my face against the wood, pretending that it was Li's chest, that he would wrap his arms around me and lift me out of here.

Or just hold me tight until this was all over, and he got what he wanted — me with him, trapped here, forever.

"This place wasn't just yours," I sobbed into the gushing water, the encroaching darkness, bashing my fists into the wood just to hear something solid. I raised my voice, defiant. "Do you hear me? This was my dream, too! I could make it and unmake it! Without me it fell apart, and you knew that." My thin voice folded in on itself until it was a pinprick in an ocean of abandon. "But it wasn't my only dream, Li." I wasn't alone, and when I turned I expected him.

The lady from the river of Shalott stood on the water's surface, ruined flesh hanging off her, white hair tangled in her dead eyes as she looked at me and pointed up.

I turned and gazed at the rose window painting. I shut my eyes. "It wasn't my only dream," I repeated defiantly. "And you can't have them all."

The rose painting flashed into glass.

And the undulating torrent that exploded through the panes moaned as it surged upon me, the great tsunami filling the library in an instant, crushing my body against the Fable Door—

—and bursting it wide open, launching me, and an entire lake, out the front door. Books and shelves and the debris of our dreams tumbled after me, the wave soaking and mangling the solid earth as the debris and I met it, face first.

．。●○●

"Ash?"

Everything still swam, still tasted like a mixture of bile and fresh water. Someone was shaking me, and that name, that name that was so perfectly mine, floated on the periphery of my coming back into the world.

"Ash, wake up!"

I jolted and coughed up a lungful of water. The air was bright and clean, and I sucked at it greedily.

A bird flitted by. It was not made of paper.

"Did you sleep here all night? How did you—" It was Tabitha. She looked as though my waking had struck a high-pitched chord of relief behind her eyes.

I touched her face, her hair. "Tabs." I blinked; Paul was close at hand, the rising sun shaded behind his cropped head. I sat up, still bleary and perplexed. I was on the library's porch, and looming over me was the chained-up and tamed Fable Door. I looked back at Tabitha, my resolve breaking as I collapsed with my head on her chest.

"Oh, Tabs," I sighed into her shirt. "I had the worst dream."

DATE
ISSUED TO
CHAPTER THIRTEEN
CHAPTER FOURTEEN
PROPERTY OF
TREADE
PUBLIC LIBRARY

I had only been gone the night, even though it had felt like weeks in the library, and I felt years older. Tabitha and Paul didn't bother asking any questions, and I would have been too spent to field them. They got me home somehow; from there I called the hospital to check on Mum. She was stable but tired, and I could visit her later. Tabs and Paul fed me, and tried to coax me to take a shower, to relax, but I was too unspeakably anxious to be anywhere near water. They installed me on the sofa and opened all of the windows, airing out the empty rooms. It was sunny and silent, and cresting on the horizon was a thunderhead that was purple and pregnant with storm. For now I shied away from the idea of the rain and stared intently at the slanting rays that struck the earth. Things that had gone unseen for these last days were clarifying themselves like an Impressionist painting; soft, details skewed, but they still had form. Still had light. I clung to that, at least, and that I could see faces again, even though I was ashamed to look at them.

Tabitha took my hands and pressed a mug of tea into

them. I couldn't look back at her, guilt the only thing left since the briar patch inside me had shrivelled up and snapped apart like weather-worn bracken. For now I couldn't tell which was worse: that I had abandoned everything that was true and real for a momentary dance in a dream, or that I let it consume the heart in me and hurt the people that would have done everything for me had I only asked.

I still saw Li's face above me when I shut my eyes, and it said, *I'm sorry, but this is the only way.* There was love there, too, warped and cracked as it was. I shuddered.

Tabitha cuffed me under the chin. She smiled, sadly, but she was solid, ready to catch me. "Do you want to talk about it?"

"No," I replied, instantly. If I told them, it might break the spell, and a part of me still wanted to find Li, to ease the creases of his soul and assure him this wasn't his fault. But I couldn't keep shutting them out.

Paul sighed, his pale complexion wearing the same weariness that mine did, that Tabitha's did. They were all right there, sharing my grief in their own particular ways. "We tried and tried to call you, Ash," he said. "But you always seemed so far away. At first we thought it was something we did."

I curled into the corner of the sofa, trying to make myself small enough to disappear. "I know. I was . . . I *was* far away. And it's my fault. I'm sorry."

Tabitha sat next to me. "We didn't even know your mom was sick. Why didn't you say anything?"

I didn't know either. No. I truly think I did know, all along — I just didn't want to see it. I didn't want to see a lot of things. I fretted with my hands, staring deep into them. Tabitha clasped hers over mine.

Tears threatened at the corners of my eyes. I had pushed my

friends so hard over the precipice of my own gain, and yet they'd
climbed back up when it had broken me. I did not deserve this.

"I'm so sorry, you guys. I'm *so sorry.*"

Paul knelt beside me, placing a Polaroid into my lap. "We
. . . looked at the canvas. Sorry, Ash. But after I saw that, I figured that's where you'd been going."

The photo was a crisp and beautiful take of the library,
right from the front. I traced my fingers over the details,
trying to press past them and see inside. It had been hidden
behind the painting of my defiant princess — I knew that she
wouldn't keep my promise, but she had never lied to me.

"I got inside," I blurted through my tears.

Paul hesitated, looked at Tabitha, looked at me. "Did you
— what was in there?"

Li's eyes, his movements. My circus performer, ringmaster,
and clown. My own Hook, my Lancelot. My fellow wisher,
fellow dreamer. Magician and phantom saviour boy, who
could make whimsy out of paper, an aviary out of his breath.
In our castle of dreams and promises, stories and paper skies,
of water and whispers and a grey woman whose intentions
were still unclear to me. We had skipped the light fandango
over a boundary between worlds, and we lost ourselves trying
to cling to it.

Could I tell them? Could they ever know? I owed them this
much.

"I . . . I left my bag there," I stiffened. "I can show you."

. ˳ ● ○ ●

I slept like I was sick. It wasn't real sleep, just the idea of it. But
every time I slipped into even a three-minute, uncomfortable

slumber, there he was, in my blood, moving inside me and taking over my bones, trying to pull me back.

I missed him, but I feared him. So I stayed awake. Paul and Tabitha stayed the night with me after I'd come back from the hospital, and, in an effort to emulate the childhood that had been so important to us, we camped out on the living room floor — a protective circle of bodies to ward off whatever still gripped me. Rain *plik*ed against the windows like fingernails, like someone trying to get in. I watched the shapes of the water and the light brace against the ceiling, and fell deeper into a spiral of half-sleep. The hidden room that even Li couldn't see, the drowned woman that showed me the way out of my rabbit hole. The scarred painting and the bubbling wallpaper.

I thrust fully awake in the dark, careful not to wake either of my friends as my pulse beat a war drum in my ears. I glanced at their sleeping bodies — my loyal, unquestioning friends, who were giving more of themselves to me with every shallow breath. I wondered what they were dreaming now, wondered why I'd never asked.

I absently traced a circle on my palm, the palm that had bled but hadn't; touched my mouth that had kissed Li so many times, or dreamed that it had. I didn't know what I wanted anymore. He had tried to pull me under into the folds of our world — his world? — and had hurt me to do it. But I still wanted to see him again, to be a part of it.

Even though he was long gone.

· ○ ● ○ ●

The road to the library today was paved with possibility. I spent the walk thinking of what I would tell Li, steeling

myself against what the library had in store once I crossed
back into it. I kept everything inside as we dipped down the
hill, past the baseball diamond, through the fence and the field
of tall grass, through Wilson's Woods, until there we were.
Tabitha and Paul watched me, expectant, as I stared up at the
untouched rose window, spreading its petals towards the sun
as it was choked out by the rain clouds. The window. It was
still there. And so was the Fable Door. Nothing had changed.
"It's just around the back," I muttered, leading the way. It had
never felt this still before as I approached the porthole and
pushed away the debris. The library slouched on its founda-
tions, walls resting paper-thin like an abandoned wasp's nest.
It had given up the fight against the earth, had lost all protest,
its chained and boarded maw slack with submission. It was
deader than I could've imagined. But that didn't haunt me.

Managing through the porthole was not difficult, but gathering the will and courage to do it was. To come back here
had taken everything, and without Tabs or Paul it wouldn't
have happened. They followed, awed that I had been so ingen-
ious a trespasser, and silent on the topic that I had kept this
from them. Finally, we were doing what we had always promised; we went in together. One last adventure.

There were no lights here now, artificial or not. Dim sunlight through the grimy rose window was the only means to
show us the truth.

It was empty inside, and cramped, much smaller than the
outside had been telling us all these years. But here it was,
an absolute void. No shelves, no books, no ladders, no clock.
No stories or tomes or an open-handed boy to offer them.
Just an endless chasm of good intentions, gutted and hope-
less, pigeons fluttering uselessly from their ramshackle roosts

as my flashlight passed over them. There was a second level, half-built and collapsed. Part of the roof was caved in where our Terrarium Room should have been. A stringy rat darted into the shadows. Garbage, droppings, animal bones, and beer cans littered the floor.

I felt my blood surging in my ears. *No. It had been real. I touched it. I felt it. The wood, the walls, the water. It had been right here.* My brain backpedalled on itself, trying to resolve the difference between yesterday and now. The two refused each other like depolarized magnets. I swallowed and tried to calm my shaking hands, pulse quickening. All of it an illusory, empty mirage. Panic. Where was Li? Where could he be hiding when there were no crevices left to keep him? Had he been here at all?

Tabitha and Paul were mystified, but disappointed. They had thought more of this place, too. I had thought so much of it that it had nearly closed me off from the world.

Oh, God.

"Li!" I called, unable to control it, the name a sharp missile that struck the darkness and struck me back. *"Li!"*

Paul rounded on me. "Ash, who are you—" But I had taken off, flashing my light in every possible corner until I stumbled and fell. Tabitha chased to my side to help me up but I batted her away, dragging myself to my feet and looking down at what had tripped me: the deer clock, split and ruined on the dirty floor, looked to me with broken countenance. I let my fingers find the edge, content that I had found something from my dreamscape. It *had* been real.

"Please, Li!" I shouted with choked fervour into the dark, my breathing hitched and wanting ferocious. "I'm sorry, Li, I'm sorry! Please come back! Make it all come back!"

I saw something, something fleeing. Was that his shadow taking off, back around to a caved-in corner? I turned and tried to chase it, but Tabitha had her hand wrapped firmly around my forearm. I wanted to rail against both of them, but when I saw their faces I bit back my protest. "There's nothing there," Tabitha soothed.

I toed the splintered, warped floor. I pictured us lying there, watching the clouds we'd made. The memory bubbled and burst. "He's gone."

"Who?"

I looked at both of them, and for the first time in weeks, I gave them honesty. "I don't know." I never had. Not really. And now I certainly wouldn't.

We left the dark place behind, its wreckage and disgrace in my wake of mourning. But just as we were to slip through that little exit again, there it was, tucked in the corner. My bag, sitting on the toppled table that hid the porthole. It was the library's last gift, last means of redeeming itself, and as I reached for it, I saw Li clutching my picnic basket and letting the world cave in around him. He thought I had left him. And this time, he had left me. We had lied to each other. A fair trade.

. ° ● ○ ●

I climbed the stairs to my bedroom and quietly shut the door behind me. The light from the grain elevator flooded over my bed, and over my rumpled bag that I had left there. I lifted it to my chest and clung to it, hugged it hard, and tried to will it to become a part of me. I missed him. I missed what we had made. He must have left the bag for me, which meant he touched it last. He must have known I'd come back, and he must have been ashamed. This was the only truth I was willing to accept; otherwise, none of it had been real, none of it had been ours. None of it, including Li himself.

I felt a horrible knot expand in my chest. It was confusion and disappointment and anger. I pitched my bag across the room, watching it smack and topple my Polaroid Princess canvas and the easel I'd left her on. Polaroids fluttered and danced in the air like anxious moths. The contents of the bag scattered, and something big tumbled towards me.

A book.

The silver book.

Its cover winked at me, and there was nothing to stop me from picking it up now, from finding out why it had been following me all this time. The Polaroids came to rest on the carpet, and I reached past them for the book — but out of the corner of my eye, I saw a wet mark spreading towards me from the other side of the room, behind the toppled canvas. I looked up and saw her standing there. I tripped back, slamming into my closed bedroom door.

"No," I hissed. "How can you be here?"

The woman bent down and picked up the book, crossing into the grain elevator's floodlight and dripping all over my things. She was so thin that her bones threatened to tear her threadbare skin, punch holes through her nightgown. She was grey and ruined, but her milky-white eyes were steady on me. If she was still here, then there was something left of the library in this world, there had to be. I flattened as far as I could against the door as she drew closer, and closer, until she was just an arm's length away. Maybe she was here to drag me back and drown me properly, here on Li's behalf. I steeled myself for the blow.

I could smell water rot as she leaned in close, fastening something wet and cold around my neck. She pulled back and I opened my eyes as she lifted the medallion in her palm, admiring it. Her face seemed to change, seemed to relax into a sadness I hadn't noticed earlier. Then she let the medallion drop, and in the gulf between us, she offered up the book, spread the pages, and showed me. They were blank.

I stared. "I don't—"

She pushed it into my hands, insistent. She was so close now that I could see every wilted hair on her arms, each birthmark on her hands . . . and something else, something white, scratched into her skin. The longer I looked at the scratches, the clearer they became. They were words, written in a wispy cursive. They started rippling on the surface of her skin, travelling down her arms and onto the pages, which bled with the words, with dates, with a signature. It was a journal. Hers.

"*Read*," she whispered in her familiar, watery dulcet.

I cleared my throat. I read the first entry. And I went back, back . . . until my bedroom was gone, and I was somewhere else.

"You had rheumatic fever when you were a girl, didn't you?"

The cold metal of the stethoscope chest piece sends a chill into her bones. She replies between obedient breaths, "That's right. Mother prayed and drew the fever out of me after a week. It was very saint-like of her."

He pauses for a while to listen intently to her heart. "And you've had chronic strep infections, I do know that." He is quiet again.

She does not like where this is going. She nods. "Yes."

"I wish we didn't have to see each other under these circumstances," sighs the doctor, getting to his feet and pulling his stethoscope out of his ears. She waves him off, trying to smile.

"You know me, coming up with excuses just to get you to come for tea," she coughs, even a joke coming as an effort.

He marks something down on his chart, coming to her side while she relaxes on the red velvet chaise by the window. "You've been feeling poorly for a while now, haven't you, Moira?"

Her smile falters as her attention wanders around the grand room. They had lived in this house on Wellington Crescent for so long now, but in the daze of having collapsed earlier, it seems foreign, untouchable. Empty. "I wouldn't say a while," she replies, hesitant. This only draws a sigh from the weary doctor, a man who has known her and her history longer than anyone else in Winnipeg. He had even delivered her son, seen the deepest parts of her physical body. She cannot hide a lie from him.

"It's just stress, Erik," she reassures him, patting his arm weakly. "There's been so much of it going around, I was liable to catch it eventually."

Erik's gaze falls to her hand, and he puts his own hand over it in turn. "I'm sorry about your loss, Moira. David's passing was so sudden."

Eyes sharpening, she draws her hand away and folds her arms

against her chest, turning so that she might look out at the terrac
"Sudden. No. Not really."

In the midst of packing up his things, Erik hesitates. "It was a heart attack at his offices, wasn't it?"

Her smile is cruel as she breaks his question in half. "That's an apt euphemism for alcohol poisoning, don't you agree?" Her face flushes and her neck grows hot, eyes filling as she watches the gardener outside mill back and forth between her flower beds.

Erik stays quiet as she carries on. "I was advised to make his death as sympathetic as possible. For the company's sake, you see — the papers and the investors, both, want a martyr. *He was alwa, working late at his offices, said many of his colleagues*, even thoug it really should have read, *he was always obsessed with his work, and drinking made the disappointment of his family easier to bear.*

"Moira . . ."

She pricks the tears away on a fingernail and turns back to him, dry eyed and stiff. "I expect this to remain in doctor-patient confidence." She gives him a pallid grin, as if her mouth is looking for the humour in the truth.

"The confidence of a *friend*," he corrects. He takes off his glasses, smiling at her with the all the pleasantness of a reaper.

"What's the verdict?" she finally asks, staring back out the window, even though she already knows.

He puffs out his cheeks and exhales. "Your blood pressure is incredibly low, Moira. You're weak and you've been experiencing episodes of syncope or fainting, shortness of breath, chronic fatigue. I see it in a lot of my patients with a history of rheumatic fever or related infection. The after-effects are degenerative, usually rising in severity after a few years due to the weakened heart, but your body has held out for over twenty-five years, which is remarkable . . ."

Her chest rattles as the tears spring and spill afresh. "Please, Erik. Don't sugar-coat it for my sake."

He sighs, looking straight at her. "I'm sorry, Moira. It's only going to get worse from here."

She knows her heart hasn't failed her yet, because she's still able to draw breath. "How long?"

The hardwood floor creaks as he rocks on the balls of his feet. "You're a strong woman, and it's hard to tell. Six months. A year. Longer. But not . . . very long."

Her eyes score the room, looking anywhere but at him. Then they fall to the occupied piano stool on the other side of the room.

"There's nothing you can administer?" comes the third voice from the piano. The doctor turns to it, eyebrows raised.

"I can certainly prescribe something to ease the pain, to make the days a bit better for her." He pens a prescription, leaves it on a nearby side table, and crosses the room to the door. "Unfortunately, there's no procedure that could repair her weakened cardiac valves. I'm sorry."

Moira buries her face in her hands, trying to wipe away the shame of her outburst, of her fear. She pats her cheeks. "We were going on a trip to our cottage next week. To get away from the city, from all the people. Can we still do that?"

Erik hesitates at the door. "Your cottage is in . . . Treade, correct? That town just outside of Brandon?"

She nods, face splotchy with emotion but with all the expectation of a child about to be denied a rare gift. He nods. "Yes, but I wouldn't advise you taking too many trips back and forth between your cottage and the city. The extra stress won't do you any favours at this stage."

The occupant of the piano stool gets to his feet and settles on the edge of the chaise, next to Moira. "Maybe we can stay there for a few months? The lake air would do you some good. You have always loved that lake."

The doctor nods, giving them one more sad smile. "Sounds like fine idea." And he leaves them alone.

Moira looks at her son, levelling him with worried eyes that she reserves for him. "Lionel. You can't afford to go to Treade with me, alone spend months away from the city. You have . . . responsibiliti to Jovan Grain now. Responsibilities you have to fulfil."

He takes her hand and cups it to his heart. "Responsibilities," he repeats. "You are my responsibility, Mama. Always have been." He smiles through his own tears. "I'm going with you. As long as takes. I won't let you go that easily."

DATE
ISSUED TO
CHAPTER FIFTEEN
PROPERTY OF
TREADE
PUBLIC LIBRARY

I stood in a wide, beautiful parlour whose decor sang of a thousand yesterdays. The sun peeled in through the open window, and there was a terrace and beautiful gardens beyond it. There was a woman sitting on our familiar library sofa, a dying woman, but she was not quite at death's door – her pallor was that of someone too determined to let go. The woman on the sofa was not the ruined grey spectre that haunted me, bidding me to read her story out loud — but I knew she would become her, and that I'd soon find out how.

In the scene with the not-yet-spectred woman, her son was at her side, whispering her a promise. Holding her hand to his chest. I clenched the silver diary so hard I feared my fingers would break. *Lionel*, she had called him.

But to me, he was always *Li*.

The drowned Moira standing watchful and sad beside me leaned in and turned the page. And the dates sped on. May, June, July, 1929.

I travelled down, down, down into the darkling cavern of her memory, her life with him in a Treade I had never suspected could exist. It startled my eyes with the sepia grain of an old photograph, and the crystal clarity of the truth, all at once. I saw him again at her bedside, and I glanced over his shoulder to unwind the meaning of the drawings in his hands — of the journal that had been the incubator for the library all along. Saw the heartache and misery that drove them from the suffocating city to find some peace, so they might forget all their miseries and build their world anew. I passed through days and nights, saw the library rise from the forest like a Titan, unchanged. Li was a poet, a dreamer like me, but he dreamed his way to this place — not out of it. He wrote his name in the sand at Lake Jovan, watched it wash away, and felt a part of this place. He was so close to me, but I could not shape this story, Moira's story, in the way we had shaped all the countless others that came before. I could only stand around, helplessly watching it unfold in front of me. I reached out to touch him, but then the page turned, and we were at a gorgeous party, replete with flapper dresses and swell gentlemen. Li was about to make a choice that would change his life — that would punctuate what dreams he had left. He would have nothing of it, and so I followed him out of there.

He had been drinking, and he kept drinking. He had a mickey on him that he had been hesitant to fill, but he had wanted it just in case he lost his nerve that night. He walked. And he walked. He was tall and strong and I had to hurry to keep up with him. "Where are you going?" I whispered. He looked over his shoulder for a second, as if he had heard me. But he kept walking.

The page turned. We had arrived at the rocky hill above Lake Jovan, even though Li usually favoured going down to the beach. He stood on the cliff that Tabitha, Paul, and I had come to, throwing treasures into the rocks below, pretending

that this was our battleground, marking it as ours. But it had
been his first.

It was dark, the sky a bruised purple as the sun set totally.
Li sat down on the edge, one knee up, the other leg dangling,
and he sat there a long time, thinking, squinting into the distance, trying to puzzle out how he had come to this point. He
took out his flask one more time, and when I thought he was
going to take another drink, he hurled it into the water. He
was taking a last look at the life of dreaming he was going to
have to give up for the sake of the business he hated, but he
would not make the mistakes of his father. He would do this
for his mother, and he would build a beautiful life for himself,
for her. Until the bitter end.

After a while, after preparing himself, he got to his feet.
But he got up too quickly, the spirits he'd been drinking all
night going to his head. He pivoted and his ankle bent, and he
tripped backwards, arms wheeling.

He disappeared over the edge before I could reach out and
pull him back.

"No!" I screamed, diving to the ground. I watched the lake
swirl up to meet him, and he was gone. Swallowed.

"*No*," I whispered under my breath, burying my face in my
arms. I had lost him all over again.

"It looks so easy, doesn't it?"

I looked up. A page had turned in the midst of my grief.
Moira was standing beside me, hand extended, eyes trained
on the water. Her flesh had resolved into a pink liveliness, her
hair set in curls so blonde they made sunlight envious. She
was beautiful, even though her bones still looked like a fragile
bird's — but this was a Moira I hadn't seen yet, one that wasn't
plagued by dying, or death.

I stood up, looking at the water along with her, crossing my arms and pushing them into my chest. The biting wind off the lake was merciless in this half-memory world, but Moira felt none of it.

"He's been alone all this time," she said, "waiting to be pulled out of the dark."

The surface of the water was being sliced by the wind, growing darker the longer we stood there. "You tried to go down there, to find him," I said.

She pulled her arm back to herself, taking a step forwards. "I tried, yes. But we died in separate directions. He fell through a door, trapped in the sanctuary I had built to keep him safe, keep him happy. But when I jumped, the door was closed, and I couldn't reach him." She finally looked at me, her eyes exactly *his* eyes, like two glinting chips of untouchable ice. "Until you went in, until you reached him. It was like the door opened a crack. And I thought *I* could reach him through *you*."

I shivered, still unsure as to what part I had to play in this. "I can't reach him," I quivered. "I don't know what makes me so special now, what made me see him at all."

"There are lines drawn between us that I could not cross," she went on. "He still had half a foot in this world, and I was a shadow on it. But you," her bright, cold eyes softened, "you found your way to him. You heard his heart calling. I think you always did."

I remembered the years of visiting the library before knowing what it was, of lingering and hanging back to look over my shoulder at it, feeling like it needed me.

Moira tapped me out of my memories. "But this last door is sealing up quickly, and neither of us have managed to pull him back out again. There isn't much time left."

"So this . . ." I caught a glimpse of the water, saw it undulating in a slow circle, a quiet maelstrom brewing. *This was the last way back to him.*

"We are lost without our names, without the stories that we scratched into the surface of our hearts. His story is trapped in the water. I tried to use the lake as a means of getting through to him, but his grief twisted it, summoned it when he was desperate, and he tried to use it against you. But without his name or his story, he cannot break from it."

She took me by the hand. She was so warm, and she smiled. "Moira. That was *my* name." We stood over the water, and once again she grasped the medallion around my neck, and she turned it over, the name *Lionel* burning red and new out of the sea of scratches and scuffs. "But once upon a time, Moira had a boy. He needs his story back. Wherever it went. And you need to tell it, just as you told me mine."

I kicked a loose stone from the edge of the hill. It tumbled end over end and, before it could hit the water, the lake rose up to take it.

"Is this just another dream?" I sighed. "Or will I die, too?"

Moira laughed and clenched my hand tighter. Together, we stood at the edge like it was a diving board. "It's all just a dream, Ashleigh. This life." I bent at the knees, ready to spring, and she finally let go of my hand. "We all wake up from it, eventually."

I dove.

End over end. The rushing air ripped at my hair, at my skin. The water climbed up and up and up, and in its mighty fist, it towed me down. And I thought of Li instantly, felt like I could see his fall for myself as I experienced my own: it was such a long way down from the rock hill into Lake Jovan.

How he must have smashed headlong into it. How the water must have embraced him as it dragged him down, drawing him into a world where he would have to drown again and again, his story scarred underneath his flesh and known by no one. It took him to a place where he would forget the world and it would forget him, too.

Then I felt him well up in my blood. Felt his story scar my own skin as I kept swimming deeper and deeper and deeper until the bottom of the lake came into view . . . but it wasn't the bottom at all. It was, at first, a darkness, but it rippled into shape — it was the library, as though I was coming at it through the ceiling. It rippled back and forth, first the darkness, then the library, unable to decide if it should resolve itself as I pressed against the membrane of those fragile planes. I was diving right back into it, and I reached, until I heard someone call out in my head like a rushing, desperate wave. His voice. His beautiful, frightened voice that, even though I had only heard it through Moira's memories, was weaving through my heart now. I shut my eyes and told the story over his words as I crossed over the threshold of his life.

Once upon a time there had been a boy named Lionel. He dreamed, and he dreamed . . .

And I listened.

· ∘ ● ∘ ●

Wet, wet. Woke up wet. Don't know how. A fever? I'm dreaming. Must be dreaming. Do I know this place?

It is a womb of darkness. He floats through it at first, until he lands on solid ground. He races around, arms outstretched,

rying to feel for walls. He runs for years. Finally the walls
assert shapes, forms. They climb out of his nearest memories,
and the darkness pulls back, little by little.

*Somewhere I've been before, somewhere that's important to me and
someone else. Library. It's a library.*

He comes upon crates and crates of books and shelves. The
shelves are empty. He leafs through the books, reads them.
Reads them all to pass the time. But no one comes. His
thoughts dance around in my head, and I follow them, follow
him, as he passes his time in the library. I'm *his* ghost now.

*Hit my head, maybe, so confused. I'm sure I've fallen. Almost a
haze in front of my face. Can't see things clearly. There are books
everywhere. No one else here, still. Summer, it was summer. Feels
like it is a distant dream. Tried leaving this place once or twice.
Doors are locked from the outside. How did I get in here? People
will be coming soon, I'm sure of it. Hearing trains passing by every
now and again. Am I lost? Head isn't any better than before. Don't
feel as though I slept last night. Went downstairs and realized that
all of the crates were gone, the shelves filled with books. When did
that happen? Must've fallen hard. Can't make sense of anything.
Only logic is in the books. Find myself stopping when I'm holding
them. Feeling like I've gone through them before. Heard them from
someone, maybe. Maybe. Maybe I'm here to wait for who showed me
the books. I know I should keep waiting. Will stay and wait. Yes.
Can be patient. Got a lot to keep me busy. As long as I can read, I'll
be fine. It's cold. So cold. Cold. Help, please help. There is a drip in
the ceiling, in the walls. Can't find the source, can't hear rain outside. Water. So much water.*

I swim in the wake of his thoughts as they tremble in and out of him, one after another. I still feel the water pressing on me on all sides, and soon it starts to become *too* heavy. But I have to let the story wash over me, too. And people did come to the library. Eventually. I watched and waited with him, tried to offer some comfort, but gave none.

Workmen. Didn't come inside, only outside. Boarded up the windows, chained the door. Shut out the sunlight. It's dark. Hammers are in my head. Closing up, making it leave, gone, gone. Why? Varnish smell is still strong on the glossy wood of the banisters and tables, clock is still ticking on the farthest wall. Glass is new in the windows clear and new as crystal. Got up, called out, waved my arms, but they did not turn or see. Gone so fast. Run to the upstairs, to the attic. There is one window here I won't let them board up. Watched them speeding away. Started to talk to myself, read out loud. It comforts. Eases. Yes.

His emotions wash over me, his suffering, his loneliness. I can feel his thoughts more than hear them. As time passes, seasons shifting, the town beyond growing and changing, the library decays. The idea of it falls into ruin, all around him, and he barely sees it. Darkness flickers in. I try gathering him in my arms. He feels none of it.

So cold. Can't count the days. Don't sleep. Stop. Quiet. Tighten. Shut your eyes, stare into dark space. Dream of something comforting, flashes of something I'm sure I know but can't prove in front of me. Orange sunshine filtering through trees, a garden and a swing, a woman in white. She's smiling and holding her arms out, then gone. She looks so happy. Open my eyes reaching out for her in

*he emptiness. There is no one. Only she, the vision woman, woman
n white, would be right here.

Time goes on. He talks to himself, tries to get the thoughts
out. But after a while, the words don't come anymore. He
loses them, loses parts of himself. He soon comes to terms
with the fact that maybe he no longer inhabits the world as he
once did, so the conventions of that place fall away. His voice
fails. His words die. Watching this . . . no, absorbing it into
myself. It's more difficult to bear than the feeling that I have
come so deep that I won't ever breach the surface again.

*Hard to speak anymore. No one to talk to anyway. At least thinking
is possible still. Wrench. Glare. Squint hard enough. There.
Something in my heart jumps. Think I'm about to remember something. Names. Where do they come from? Have one? I have one. Do.
Have to. Everyone has. Something around my neck. Name. A medallion. Saint marked. Name on the back. Lionel. St. Anthony on the
front. Lost things. Need a name to find the lost things. Keep it close,
so close, closest. Can keep waiting if I have it. Only give it to her, the
one I'm waiting for. Only for her. Who?*

He forgets his life. Forgets what it feels like. His loneliness and
despair shape him into a creature that barely inhabits thought.
I try to whisper in his ear the memories that Moira showed
me, tell him that he was happy once, that he was real and
breathed in the same world I came from. I keep swimming
further and further into this with him, one day, twenty years,
seventy years later. My lungs are ready to burst, and I can feel
my head going under, but I want to ride this out with him.
Need to. I try to curl up next to him, but he is still so far away,

and getting farther as I take on every shuddering thread of this part of his story into my drowning body. His thoughts, his desperation, spill out freely, start setting a grainy buzz into my head. His thoughts overlap so many times that they melt into a horrible, pinging frequency. I swim as deep as I can, the pressure of the never-ending memories crushing me. He has nearly lost what little there is left of him. He can barely keep his thoughts strung together, anymore. They start spinning in an endless caterwauling carousel, and I cling to it desperately, shutting my eyes as the carnival ride speeds up.

Lionel. Lionel. Lionel. Lionel. I am Lionel. Dizzy. Wish I could sleep when is she coming the name on the medallion, it's faded, getting colder hands freezing still can't get dry, i miss her whoever she is no one here and wish there was but know there won't be for a long time tried reading but that started hurting tried getting out today but they barred the doors doors yes windows too maybe nothing was supposed to get in or out. trapped i'm alone no one's looking for me no one will need to cry but it's hard. Always been this way yes never different if this is hell, then this is the most clever of punishments reading is harder than it was starting to lose whatever i had left when i got to this place i think ive always been here. cant stop waiting for her even if ive always been here forgotten most things but not about her. her face is blurry and hard to remember. Her eyes, eyes, so full and yes, those eyes but i know shes coming back for me. eyes are watering, wanting so bad to shut but cant looked out the window today, tiny, tiny window. saw children that are made blurry by the years they stare up at the library, at the window, searching, talking my voice was nothing, so i hit the glass, hit it hit it hard but they didn't look, didn't hear, two of them left one stayed behind staring. wonder if she could hear could see. keep seeing the three

they're eager to get in, like some of the others but i know they cant
they can try but won't get in. they look different, changed, older.
didn't i just see them? banged and banged the girl turned her head
hung back then she was gone. so weak. my name my name my name
is my name is my name my name is lio li li li li li li li has to be it. got
to keep it with me on a piece of paper. its gone. ive lost it the paper
my name i am nothing without a name

The carousel stops suddenly. I wince my eyes open. It is the night of the storm, the storm that brought me here in the first place. Li is drowning as the library fills up with his sadness, the water overcoming him as he settles, limp, devastated. The water is rising, but he refuses to move against it, to rally. I try to shake him, but he is resigned to his fate. He wants this as he lies soaked, head to toe, in his own misery.

The rain. I can hear it pattering, the torrent raging outside, and something old and splintered snaps like internalized lightning. Li's eyes snap open. I can't hear his thoughts anymore because they have calmed, have settled. The water recedes, ebbs away, as he leaps to his feet. I only have enough left in me to career in Li's steps as he registers the scream echoing through the library, my familiar, terrified cry making him bolt. I see him on the landing, diving, diving, sliding for the space between the banisters. His hand plunges into empty air, and just as I feel like my body can't take it anymore, can't tell this story to the end, my eyes are going black, black—

—and he grabs my wrist in the past and the present.

And he pulls me out of the water.

DATE
ISSUED TO
CHAPTER FIFTEEN
CHAPTER SIXTEEN
PROPERTY OF
TREADE
PUBLIC LIBRARY

My insides uncoiled, my heart contracted, valves pumping. Life. Air. Things I took for granted, but they were working their way through my body, kneading the light back into me. I opened my eyes — I was being dragged up onto a plinth that was sticking out of the water. No, not a plinth. A toppled bookshelf. I blinked and rolled my head to look around; the water was draining away into an unseen hole in the earth — no. In the library floor. Because that's where I was, the library, only . . . the walls were crumbling, quietly, and without ceremony. The rose window came free of the brick and plaster that had held it aloft, and it dissipated into grains of crystal. The walls became clots of sand, blowing away on a lake wind, and shelves that had been swept up in the storm were now firmly planted in the ground, the trees that they were made of coming back to roost, in a way.

When the walls were gone, I realized there was someone next to me, strong hands on my shoulders, trying to shake me out of the daze. With a massive *ping,* my hearing swung back, and I could hear his voice.

"Are you all right?" he said. "Are you . . ."

The shadows finally let him go, let me see his face, his cloudy-grey eyes soft and relieved. Supporting me with an arm, Li got me to sit up as he rubbed my back.

"I was afraid I'd lost you," he chided. "I've never pulled anyone out of a lake before. Couldn't be sure that I was doing it right. How'd you get down here, anyway?"

I was so happy to see him, so breathless and bursting to be in his arms, but before I could answer him, his next question took the wind straight out of me, again.

"What's your name?"

My face fell as I searched his in earnest. He didn't know me. "I'm . . ." I swallowed, throat thick. "I'm Ash."

"*Ash*," he repeated, rolling my name on his tongue like a gumball. He smiled. "Sounds like something out of a fairy tale."

I tried to smile, but it didn't last. "Yeah" was all I could say. I had been waiting so long to really talk to him, to hear him say my name and feel it course through me. But this was painful. I looked away from him and saw that we were on the beach of Lake Jovan, back when it had been clean and beautiful and loved. Jovan. His lake. The water was so calm that it looked like green glass. I pulled myself together and managed to climb off the bookshelf, the sand supple beneath my bare feet. Li followed me.

"Do you know *your* name?" I asked, suddenly whirling on him. That caught him off guard, and he hesitated, and in that moment I thought I had failed, but something glinted at his throat. My hand shot to my neck, but it was bare. Absently he fingered the medallion dangling at his chest, eyes faraway before he blinked, shook his head, and held out his hand.

"Of course I do. I'm Lionel." He shook my hand gently,

warmly, clasping it in both of his. "I had honestly begun to think I was the only one who came down here." He surveyed the lake, full of pride. "My mother and father and I used to walk here when I was a little kid. I'd fill my pockets with smooth stones, and we'd skip them 'til the sun went down." His brow furrowed, and he toed the sand. "It's funny. I've been trying to get back here for some time. I only just found it when I saw you in the water."

I flushed, tucking a stray hair behind my ear and leaning down to scoop up a stone. It felt so real. "Glad I could help," I muttered, turning the stone over in my hand. He leaned down and took it from me, and in an expert flick of his wrist, it skipped across the lake ten times and vanished.

"I think I'm dreaming," he decided, eyes still trained on the lake, on the horizon.

I crossed my arms and considered it, feeling a bit slighted. "Who said it was *your* dream? I think it might be mine."

He laughed at that. His laugh was so full of light. I wished he had laughed more, in life. I wished that he could remember the laughter we shared in our brief one. "That's what people usually say in dreams. I guess we'll just have to go with it, until one of us wakes up and we know for sure."

I think I startled him as my hand wound its way into his and held tight. His face wavered in the screen of my tears. But this was important. "You were so alone," I said, "and I know you didn't mean to hurt me." I clasped tighter. "I forgive you, all right?"

He shut his eyes and took my other hand, pulling me close and looking down at our hands as though they were the only real thing about any of this. "You know," he murmured, "I haven't had a dream in a very, very long time." His eyes found

mine as he released my hand and chafed a knuckle under m
chin. "But I'm glad you're in this one."

"Me, too," I said. I could feel the warmth growing betwee
us, and his hands getting looser. We both looked out at th
lake. There was someone on the far shore, waving. Li nodded
but he didn't move. He didn't know what to do.

I sighed. "She's been waiting a while."

He looked between the two of us — the waving woma
on the shore and me. I was fading, but I smiled, and it fille
me up.

"Don't worry about me," I said. "We'll see each othe
again."

He smiled. "Will we?"

"Sure." I shrugged. And he let go, turning away from me
and taking one tentative step, then the next, until he was past
the shore and the tide of the water pulled back and back and
back, until there was no more lake to impede his path to the
opposite shore.

"In another dream, maybe?" he called over his shoulder.

"Yeah," I assured him.

In another dream.

In all of them.

And then the lake tide crept back in, like he had never
walked across it at all.

Moving day came as fast as summer lightning, and it felt like I was watching it go by through a prism. Tabitha and Paul helped me load the boxes into the U-Haul, and Mum passed me one last box that had been left in my room. Before I pulled the door down, something caught my eye — a pile of Polaroids kept together by a rubber band. I scooped them up, pocketed them, and hopped down to the ground.

"That's the last of it," Mum called, coughing a little before taking a puff on her inhaler. I had told her just to stick to the sidelines on this, but she had wanted to be involved — as if she hadn't just come home from the hospital. I still looked at her with relief and worry, like she was going to slip through my fingers like a bit of smoke and disappear. But not today. And not for a long time, either.

I wished there had been more to pack away, but that was the last of it. Packing had taken less effort than I anticipated. Emptying rooms and making them fresh for new lives and new stories seemed as right as leaving always had. Whereve we were going, someone else was doing the same for us.

There were a hundred goodbyes stuck in my throat as Pau and Tabitha drew me into their arms. We stayed like this fo a long time, muttering regrets and hopes and promises into this fragile triangle of our three lives. It wasn't as thougl we wouldn't see each other again after this, but change wa sweeping us up, and we were dreaming in three differen directions, as we always sort of did.

We separated, drying each other's tears. It was time. Time that finally ran its course, the hands meeting on the clock as it was rewound, about to be set into motion again. The weeks, the last days, had slipped past me like so many breezes and balled-up cellophane . . . but then again, so had the years. But we'd endure. We always did.

Mum popped open the driver's side — she would drive half the way, and I would bring us home on the last leg. This was how we wanted it to be; we wanted this leaving, this beginning to be in both of our hands. I climbed into the passenger seat.

Our car pulled out slowly, the world I had known ebbing away on the periphery. Paul and Tabitha stood there, like receding beacons on open water, waving and waving. I waved until my arm hurt, until they were pinpricks. Then we turned, and they and our house — just a house, now — were gone.

The road stretched before us, the sun climbing behind. My mother and I were two sunflowers, turning our heads towards the light, and I felt it ripple underneath my ribs as I dug in my pocket and pulled out the Polaroids.

"What are those?" Mum asked, pulling up to a stop sign.

I slipped the rubber band off. "Oh, just some pictures I took this summer."

I turned them over, readying for an onslaught of that final reverie of sadness, of memory. But nothing came. The pictures were blank. They had always been blank. Except one of them.

The library looked beautiful, that first picture I had of it, but its outline was a lot dimmer now, faded and worn. The car stopped again at the railroad tracks as the barrier went down and the warning signal blinked. I looked up, and Wilson's Woods was on the other side of the car. If I squinted hard enough, I could see workmen and their big machines milling around in there, the front ends of their rigs and cranes plunging into the walls as the library came down around them. The train flew by in a torrent. The barrier lifted. And we were on our way, again.

Li and I had passed through and into so many stories, and we had spun our own world out of the threads of the ones we tried so hard to escape. So many stories. But this one, the one that began with him and ended with me, was ours. And however fleeting or imagined, it remained solid, written in tight cursive on the undersides of our hearts and set free into the water. There it could thrive and pass through the membrane that separated this life and the other. It was there, in the depths, that there was a light.

"We're leaving," Mum had said.

Just for now, I thought.

ACKNOWLEDGEMENTS

Writing a book is a solitary effort. You hole yourself and shut out the world for months until the story is told. But it goes without saying that there will always be people on the other side of the door, cheering you on all the way no matter how long it takes or how discouraged you become along the way.

I wrote this book when I was 16 years old and had really no idea what I was doing, but knew I had a story to tell and wouldn't stop 'til it was told. I was high on praise I had been getting for years from teachers and mentors on my creative writing, and determined to tell every story that was popping into my overactive brain. Thanks first go to those teachers who never let me down: to Brenda Probetts, whose Grade 7 English class dictated I give it my all with creative writing, having to read a book and write a new piece every week for two straight years. And special thanks to Audrey Mireault, who encouraged me to go after my writing dreams post–high school no matter the cost, and who taught me the value of Manitoba literature.

Of course, you can't get very far without the loyal (and many years long) support of friends, and luckily I had one of the best vanguards at my side. Thanks to the 1st Southdale Rovers, who were always cheering even before the book was remotely a book. Many more thanks to my ChiZine Publications family (and my surrogate Toronto parents, Brett Savory and Sandra Kasturi) who drank toasts to me the day the contract was signed 'til the day I moved back to Winnipeg, and who gave me the opportunity to do my first ever (nervous as hell) author reading. And really, thanks to every damn person that has come up to me since I started anxiously mumbling that I had a book coming out — friends, family, in-laws, co-workers, peers, strangers, panel attendees . . . everyone has been nothing short of hysterically enthusiastic for my humble efforts.

Obviously, thanks to everyone at ECW for taking a chance on me, for working hard on this book, and a hundred thousand thanks to my editor, Jen Hale, who was a tireless supporter of the book from the day she yanked it from the slush pile and through the long days of Epic Revisions.

And to my parents, Patricia and Dennis, always there to not only support but help make whatever dreams I had come true at any given time. Thanks for buying me books instead of video games, Mom. And for never letting me be anything less than myself. Huge kudos go to my brother, Chris, as well, because if I hadn't watched him write and create and read voraciously at a young age, I don't know if I would've started writing as young as I did. His example really shaped me.

And then there is Peter. My rock, my foundation, my cuddler, and my reality-checker. Bless him, he read this book in its original form and was too in love with me to say it was anything less than awesome (the sweet fibber). You have been there for me for absolutely everything, beyond the work, beyond life. I hope I can write you many more stories, my love.

And to you, little reader, whoever you are. Thanks for reading. Thanks for dreaming with me.